ILLUMINATED

A Djinn Wars Holiday Novella

CHRISTINE POPE

Dark Valentine Press

ILLUMINATED

ISBN: 978-1-946435-08-8

Copyright © 2017 by Christine Pope

Published by Dark Valentine Press

Cover design by Lou Harper

Book layout by Indie Author Services

Chapter One

Cloudcroft, New Mexico, two and a half months after the Dying

SARAH WRIGHT CAST A WARY EYE AT THE SKY, sure she had seen a shadow pass overhead. Of course there was nothing to see, just as there had been absolutely nothing every other time she'd stopped in her tracks, sure that the shadow of a hawk or an eagle would turn out to be something much worse.

Maybe someday she'd stop startling at every little thing. Maybe.

Still, it didn't hurt to pause here on the top step before the entrance to the Lodge resort, to let her gaze sweep the area once more. Just in case.

The fountains that had once danced in the pond at the entrance to the historic hotel were now still, and algae had begun to bloom in the water—until the first few hard freezes came along, followed by a few half-hearted storms, ones that had brought flurries of snow, not enough to stick. It was strange; usually by the middle of December, Cloudcroft would have experienced at least a couple of decent snowstorms. But this year the snow came and went, although the cold was severe enough that the algae in the pond was long gone.

Sarah reflected that she should be gone, too, unless she wanted to be trapped up here all winter. The mild weather couldn't hold forever. Problem was, she had no idea where she was supposed to go.

Frowning, she let herself into the building and went past the reception desk, past the portrait of Rebecca, the hotel's resident ghost. The place was supposed to be haunted, but Sarah had never seen hide nor hair of Rebecca in all the time she'd spent here. Ghost stories were good for bringing in tourists, but if

Rebecca really existed, you'd think she would have made an appearance by now. Even ghosts might want some company after the end of the world.

The air was chilly—it got cold up here at the top of the world, at nearly 8,500 feet—but Sarah knew she'd only fetch another shawl or sweater if she became too uncomfortable. Luckily for her, the hotel had a good supply of wood on hand pretty much year-round, just because the tourists from the flatlands liked to see a fire going at the lodge, even at the height of summer. Even so, she was trying to be careful with the firewood, since she'd have to make it last a good long time.

Tourists. Once upon a time, they'd driven her nuts, even though it was the tourist trade that put a roof over her head. Clogging the narrow road up here to Cloudcroft, jamming her favorite restaurants, idling along while they gawked at all the sights. It had been a relief to go down the hill to Alamogordo or Tularosa, someplace where the streets were a little wider and you didn't feel as if outsiders were pressing in from all sides. Now, though, Sarah would have welcomed the most obnoxious Escaladedriving Texan. At least that way, she would have known she wasn't alone in the world.

She passed through the large lobby with its overstuffed furniture and enormous fireplace, and went out to the gazebo. In happier days, people used to get married here. Now, though, the garden and the gazebo were empty, the wind rustling in the pines, the neglected grass bare and yellow. A month ago, fallen leaves had coated the lawn, but they'd mostly blown away by this point. Those leaves had told her that time was running out. Snow came early at this elevation, most years. She had long overstayed her welcome, and knew it. One day a real blizzard would come along, and she'd be snowed in, trapped because she'd been too scared to go and see what had actually happened to the world outside Cloudcroft.

There really wasn't anything keeping her here. Lord knows the town was littered with abandoned vehicles whose former owners wouldn't be needing them anytime soon. All she had to do was find one with the keys still in it, pack up her things, drive down the mountain, and…

…and what? As far as she could tell, the

whole world was dead. No electricity. Nothing on the TV or radio. Not even anything on the ham radio setup her neighbor Kyle was once so proud of, and which still occupied the cramped spare bedroom of his small house. Thank God he'd showed her how to use it, back when she was a little girl and her father needed someone to babysit her. Kyle's grandkids were all in Abilene, so he was only too happy to spend time with Sarah, patiently explaining how the radio setup worked. She'd been fascinated, had never forgotten those lessons.

Which was why she knew no one was out there broadcasting. Or at least, they weren't broadcasting any signals she could pick up. Kyle had warned her that with the mountain peaks all around and the crazy air currents up here, the radio signals weren't always as reliable as they would be down in the flats. Still, after more than two months, you'd think she would have been able to hear something. Anything. Even a garbled transmission would have told her someone else was alive out there. And maybe that would have been enough to hold the despair at bay.

However, as far as Sarah could tell, she was

the only person left alive in the world. How that had happened, she couldn't begin to guess. Clearly, she was immune to the hideous fever that had claimed everyone else...but why? Like most of the people who lived up in Cloudcroft, she was fit enough, had spent most of her life hiking and climbing in the summer, skiing and skating in the winter. But being in shape sure hadn't saved any of her friends and neighbors.

Or, presumably, her father. He was the chef at the Lodge's restaurant, had gone down the hill into Tularosa to pick up a load of pistachios and pecans from some local farmers. At that time, there had been scattered reports of a strange sickness hitting the larger cities, but nothing to cause too much alarm. Sarah guessed now that some of those reports must have been suppressed in order to prevent widespread panic, because it had all happened so fast. A few hours after her father left, guests began keeling over while eating breakfast, or out on the golf course, or on their way to check out early because they suddenly weren't feeling well. They burned with a fever like nothing she'd ever seen before.

And then...and then their bodies turned to ash, and they were gone.

She'd been working at the reception desk because she didn't know what else to do with herself. Two years of community college completed, but not enough money to finish her degree at the University of New Mexico in Albuquerque. Besides, going off to school would have meant leaving her father alone, and she hadn't wanted to abandon him. Not when it was only the two of them, and had been for most of her life.

Anyway, he'd never come back from Tularosa. And neither had anyone else.

During those terrible two days, she'd fought the panic within her, the knowledge that she'd be next, that she'd start to burn with fever, then collapse and fade to dust, as if the fever was so hot, it ended up incinerating the very body that had generated it. Only, that hadn't happened to her. She'd survived. And now the Lodge wasn't haunted by Rebecca, the chambermaid who'd supposedly been murdered there a hundred years earlier, but by a living person.

What frightened Sarah the most, however, wasn't the empty hotel, or the abandoned town outside the Lodge. Not the silence on the radio, or the worry that, even with scrounging from every house in town and the little market down the street and the Family Dollar, she still might not have enough food to get through the winter. She hadn't ever stopped to think about how much of the modern world's food supply depended on refrigeration. The power had cut out on the third day, as though the outside world had managed to hold on for just a little bit longer than tiny Cloudcroft, and though there had been plenty of food in the hotel's freezers, Sarah hadn't been able to save it.

The weather hadn't gotten truly bad yet, but she'd lived here all her life and knew what lay in store for her. She didn't want to think about what the highway would be like with no snow-plows to come along and clear away the drifts that accumulated with every storm.

No, what really scared her were those elusive shadows at the edges of her vision, strange movements that couldn't be explained away by telling herself a bird had just flown overhead, or a sudden gust of wind had set a tree branch dancing. It could be her imagination. Sarah wanted to believe that. She was reacting to things that weren't there, simply because her brain couldn't deal with the reality of being alone in this town, alone in the world.

That had to be it. Because the alternative

was even worse than being by herself, the only person somehow lucky—or cursed—enough to have survived that hideous fever.

If she wasn't imagining things, then she feared that, crazy as it sounded, someone was watching her.

Kamal al-Sayid watched Sarah go inside the hotel and shut the door behind her. A frown was pulling at her pretty brow, and he couldn't help but notice the way she kept sending furtive glances to either side, as though she'd managed to detect his presence, had realized she wasn't quite as alone here in Cloudcroft as she'd thought.

How she was able to do such a thing, when he'd been very careful to use his djinn glamour to keep himself nearly invisible, to always remain at the very periphery of her field of vision, he was not quite sure. Part of him wanted to go to her, to explain that she had nothing to fear. He would have to do so soon enough, for he could not keep up this furtive surveillance forever. But he still wished to observe her, wanted to be quite sure he had made the right choice.

Oh, she was lovely. That fact could not be disputed. And, from what he had been able to see so far, quite resourceful as well. Each day she ventured forth from the hotel where she'd made her home and went from house to house, gathering up what nonperishable goods she could find so she might bring them back with her. Although there were plenty of abandoned cars available, she did not use any of them, but instead took an electric cart that had once been used by the hotel's staff, and which she could recharge at the end of each day, using the power provided by a bank of solar panels installed on the top of the maintenance shed.

She undertook all these missions with a pistol hanging from a holster at her hip, and a small hunting rifle sitting on the empty seat next to her. Although she must have known that she was the town's only inhabitant, it seemed she was not willing to take any chances.

Because she went about armed—a gunshot wound could not kill a djinn, but simply because something was not fatal didn't mean it wouldn't still hurt—and because Kamal was still trying to ascertain that his decision had been the correct one, he was in no hurry to approach her. His fellow djinn had already claimed their Chosen and gone on to Taos, where a community was forming, but it was not as if he'd been given any set schedule in which he must do the same. Why shouldn't he bide his time?

Some of his fellow djinn referred to him as the "scientist," which to an elemental was not precisely a compliment. However, Kamal saw nothing wrong with his approach here. Once he had gone to Sarah and made her his, then they would be bound together for all eternity. Was it so very strange that he might wish to have ample evidence of her character before making such a fateful decision?

Yes, he had observed her even before the other djinn had set the Heat—as the mortals called the fatal disease that eradicated most of their kind—upon the world. But he had watched her in her old life, watched as she did her best to be diplomatic with demanding guests at the hotel, or cooked and cleaned for her father, who spent his own days cooking for others and so was not terribly inclined to do the same when he got home from work. Observed her as she laughed with friends, or hiked alone on her days free from work, always tackling the steepest trails, the most difficult rock climbs, as though she had to prove she had the strength to face such things, even when her everyday life seemed so very mundane. It was that strength which had drawn his attention toward her, as much as her beauty.

He was glad to see that same strength now as she faced a world forever changed. From time to time, he'd seen her struggle with the possibility of leaving this place, of going down the winding road cut into the side of the mountain…but so far she hadn't. Did she fear what she would find? Or was it simply that she wanted to stay in a place which was familiar to her, even if that place was now so terribly isolated from the rest of the world?

Going down the hill would have solved nothing for her. They were all gone in Tularosa, in Alamogordo, in the Air Force base at White Sands, and over the mountains in Las Cruces beyond that. Perhaps there had been Immune in those towns and cities—in fact, Kamal knew there must have been, since the Heat was not one hundred percent fatal—but the other djinn, those who wished to see the end of humanity, would have been diligent about making sure any survivors were wiped out. If Sarah had finally decided to leave Cloudcroft and see these things for herself, then he would have been compelled to reveal himself and stop her. Until he had formally made her his Chosen, she would be fair game for those vengeful elementals, and he could not allow that.

No, it seemed he must reveal his presence in the very near future. Sarah could not have known that she was perfectly safe here, that his presence had ensured the others of his kind stayed far away. Even so, he had seen the fear growing in her, a fear not only of being trapped here with the first bad storm, which had expressed itself in the way she sometimes lingered by the sturdiest of the abandoned vehicles in town, as though trying to screw up the courage to climb behind the wheel and drive away from this place, but also the furtive glances which signaled a worry that someone was watching her, impossible as such a thing might seem.

He did not want her to be frightened.

Perhaps it would be best to go about this slowly. There was no reason to tell her he was a djinn… at least not at first. Once she got used to him, then he could tell her the truth. And eventually he would have to take her away from Cloudcroft, since it had been decreed that the Chosen and their djinn must live apart in their own communities, but he had some time.

All he needed was time enough to make her fall in love with him.

Chapter Two

ANOTHER MEAL OF CANNED VEGETABLES AND biscuits with no butter...although at least she shouldn't run out of jam or preserves anytime soon. There was no electricity, but the hotel's gas for heating water and cooking was supplied by a set of very large propane tanks, and so Sarah hoped she should be able to have hot food for the foreseeable future. The water came from a well, and so there was no shortage of that, either. Unfortunately, she had to pump it by hand—the building had a manual override on its water system—so hot showers were a thing of the past. But at least she was able to have a lukewarm bath twice a week, although the process of heating enough water on the stove to fill her bathtub was laborious, and took her more than an hour each time. Still, it could have been worse.

She ate in the lobby, in front of the fireplace. Because it was cold this evening, she'd spared a few logs and built a fire. They crackled away happily, well-seasoned after a summer and an autumn of being stored in the pile next to the maintenance shed. Covered by a set of tarps, luckily, or things would have been a lot smokier than she would have liked, even if she didn't have to worry about the smoke alarms getting tripped.

The warm firelight danced off the walls, reflected in the glassy eyes of the enormous stuffed bear that stood by one of the sets of French doors leading to the deck and the garden beyond. More than once that damn bear had scared the living crap out of her when she was distracted and not paying attention, but Sarah didn't quite want to go to the effort of carting it out of here and storing it in the maintenance shed. At least it provided a little company.

She set down her bowl of creamed corn and reached for the glass of wine that sat on the table in front of the couch. Before the apocalypse, she wouldn't have said she was much of a wine drinker—beers while out with friends had been her poison of choice—but between the cellar here at the hotel and the stock at the Noisy Water Winery in Cloudcroft's tiny downtown area, Sarah knew she was set for alcohol for at least the winter. They'd been expecting a shipment from the beer distributor when the Heat struck, and so she'd polished off the hotel's available supply in the weeks immediately following her involuntary exile.

However, she made sure never to have more than one glass of wine at a time. Just enough to take the edge off, to give her something to drink with her meager dinners besides water from the well. Then she'd re-cork the bottle and put it back on the bar, which still had a decent collection of other liquor. However, scotch and whiskey held even less appeal for her than wine, so she hadn't touched any of that stuff. It would have been so easy to spend her days drunk, trying to erase the bitter reality of her world. She didn't want to do that, though. Her father might not have been around anymore, but she still didn't want to disappoint him.

A small sip. This was a light pinot noir from Washington State, something that didn't weigh too heavily on the stomach. It probably deserved something better than creamed corn. Unfortunately, Sarah didn't have a lot of options. The forests around here had their share of wildlife, true, but she'd never been a hunter. A couple of times she'd managed to bag a rabbit with the .22 she carried around on her daily expeditions. Although the whole process of skinning the animal and getting any kind of useful meat off its bones had made her want to gag, she'd grimly forced herself through the process, knowing she needed the protein. The last rabbit had been more than a week ago, however. She'd found some canned chicken and tuna on her foraging expeditions, but she was doing her best to ration that out as well. One meal every couple of days with protein, the rest canned vegetables or fruit, and then bread or biscuits. Her cooking skills might not have been the equal of her father's, but she could manage biscuits without too much trouble.

The dancing flames in the hearth glinted off the barrel of her pistol, which now lay on top of the coffee table. Sarah found some comfort in taking it everywhere with her, even though she had no idea whether she'd be able to use it effectively if she really were attacked. Not by a human, of course; she knew she was the only human being in this town, possibly in the entire county. But there were coyotes, and maybe Mexican gray wolves, and definitely bears. She'd never seen one come anywhere near town, although she'd spotted a few while she was out hiking. Anyway, better safe than sorry, even though she feared the pistol wouldn't do much to stop a bear. It was a risk she had to take, even knowing that, if she ventured out completely unarmed and a wild animal did attack her, she wouldn't have anyone to treat her wounds afterward. She knew some basic first aid, but that only went so far. A really serious injury would kill her.

Which was also why she'd avoided rock climbing, or any hike more strenuous than was necessary to look for rabbits or squirrels to eat. Back before the world changed, she could afford to be more adventurous. It was still a drive down the hill to get to a hospital, but at least there *were* hospitals. And doctors and nurses and antibiotics and all the other good stuff.

Living alone like this was definitely no fun,

but a solitary life was still better than no life at all.

Sarah was just reaching for her glass of wine again when three loud knocks sounded at the door. Good thing she hadn't actually been holding the glass, because otherwise she would have certainly dropped it.

It had been so long since she'd heard a sound she hadn't made herself—or hadn't been made by the local wildlife—that those knocks rang in her ears like shots from a gun. Heart hammering in her breast, she reached for the pistol and slowly stood.

Maybe she was going crazy and had started hearing things. Or maybe a tree had fallen over and hit the side of the building, and it only *sounded* like someone knocking.

Pistol in hand, she began to inch toward the door to the reception area. Out of habit, she always locked it when she was here...or even when she wasn't. Safer that way, since the last thing she wanted was an adventurous raccoon to get in and cause havoc in the kitchen.

The three knocks came again. Sarah gulped back a gasp, then forced herself to continue moving forward. A horrible story came into her mind, one that her friend Alyssa had told one night back when they were in junior high and having a sleepover with a bunch of other girls from their class. Something about how a demon would knock three times, in a mockery of the Holy Trinity.

Yeah, and they're supposed to knock between midnight and three in the morning, Sarah told herself sternly. *It's probably not even eight o'clock yet.*

True, but even if it wasn't a demon…what if Rebecca the ghost had finally decided to make an appearance? Sarah might have joked to herself that she'd welcome the spirit's presence, since it would mean she wasn't alone here in the hotel, but that sort of joke was a lot more amusing in the bright light of day. Now, with the only light coming from the fireplace and one Coleman lantern turned down to its lowest setting, the prospect of a ghost roaming the halls of the Lodge suddenly wasn't funny at all.

All right. She steeled herself to open the door, trying to convince herself that the sound of the knocks had been all in her mind. And if it wasn't….

Her fingers tightened on the grip of the gun she held. Kyle's old Colt single-action pistol. More than once he'd told her proudly that the gun never jammed, had always been there for him when he needed it. She had to hope he'd been telling her the truth.

With her free hand, she reached out to disengage the bolt on the door. Now all she had to do was turn the knob.

A quick breath, and she flung the door open. A tall figure loomed over her, and she gasped and took a step back. It really *was* a bear—

Then he stepped forward, just enough that some of the dim light from down the corridor touched his face.

No, not a bear. A man.

A tall, handsome man.

At least, she thought he appeared to be handsome, although she couldn't make out too many details of his appearance because of the uncertain lighting. She stared up at him, and he said quickly, "I'm sorry. I didn't mean to frighten you." His gaze flickered to the gun in her right hand. "But I saw what I thought was a light, up here in the trees. I haven't seen anyone in months, and so—"

Sarah found her voice. "So you thought you'd better check it out."

"Yes." He hesitated, appearing to look past her and down the hallway to where the fire burned in the hearth. "Is there anyone else here?"

Maybe she should lie, tell him that yes, there was a large group of survivors staying here at the hotel. However, that kind of falsehood would be easy enough to disprove. "No," she replied, desperately hoping she wasn't making a huge mistake. "They're all dead."

His mouth tightened. "I know. That is, no one was alive down the hill, either, so I figured it would be the same up here." A pause, and then he added, "I'm Cam, by the way. Cameron Allen."

"Sarah Wright. I—" It felt so strange to be talking to someone, to realize she wasn't completely alone in the world after all. Her mouth suddenly didn't want to form the correct syllables. "Come on in. There's a fire. It's freezing outside."

"Well, not yet, but probably later tonight." As he spoke he flashed her a smile, one that made the blood rush to her cheeks.

What were the odds that her only fellow survivor would look like a male model?

She stepped out of the way so he could enter the building. Once he was inside, she closed the door, automatically locking it. "This way."

It was a little better to have him following her. That way she could avoid staring at him. Because she wanted to stare, even as her mind kept tripping over itself, trying to make some sense of his sudden appearance. Beyond that, she felt very self-conscious. Was her hair a tangled mess? Did she look like she'd just rolled out of bed? With nothing but time on her hands, she actually did spend a few minutes each day putting on some mascara and gloss, or at least tinted lip balm. Stupid, she knew. Well, maybe not completely stupid. At least the balm protected her lips from the sun and the wind.

As they came into the firelight, she could see that Cameron wore a heavy pack on his back— a real rucksack, intended for serious hiking. He paused next to the couch, undid the straps, and eased the pack down to the floor. Rubbing his shoulder, he said, "That's better."

"Where did you come from?"

A pause. Sarah noticed how his gaze moved toward the bottle of wine on the table, then shifted toward the floor, as though he didn't want to look as though he was staring.

"Do you want some?" she asked. Maybe it

had been rude not to offer him some right away. She wasn't entirely clear on end-of-the-world etiquette. "I can go get another glass—"

"That would be great. Thank you."

Yes, she supposed that hiking up the road from Tularosa would be thirsty work, especially with that heavy rucksack on his back. About all she could do was hope he'd be happy with a glass or two, wouldn't get drunk and out of hand. She might have been carrying a gun around for the past few months, but she didn't know if she'd have the guts to actually use it.

She hurried to the bar and got another glass, then came back into the lobby. Cameron had seated himself on the couch opposite the one where she'd been eating when he arrived. Now that he was closer to both the fire and the Coleman lantern, she could see his features much better. Her first impression had been correct—he really was gorgeous, with cleanly chiseled features, and longish dark hair that touched the edges of the hoodie he wore. A faint scruff of beard covered his cheeks and chin, as though he hadn't shaved in a few days, but the facial hair only seemed to enhance his looks, rather than detract from them.

"Here," she said quickly, then set down the

wine glass in front of him. She picked up the bottle of wine and filled up his glass a good deal further than halfway.

"Leave some for yourself," he said, sounding a little surprised at the amount she'd just poured for him.

"It's all right. I've already had a glass."

"If you're sure—"

"I am."

He lifted the wine glass and swirled its contents, appearing to inspect the flickers of garnet and ruby within the liquid. Then he raised it toward her. "To not being alone on this planet."

"I'll drink to that," Sarah said, although his words struck a chill within her. Clearly, he had to have come here from the flatlands. If he was toasting her for letting him know he wasn't the only survivor, then he must not have met anyone else during his journey here. She forced herself to take a sip from her nearly empty glass. "So you didn't see anyone else?"

He was in the middle of swallowing, and so he didn't answer her right away. When he spoke, his expression was solemn. "No. I'm from Roswell. No survivors there, at least as far as I could tell, and I think I walked every street in that town, looking for someone. Anyone. So I packed what I could and hit the road. I went over to Ruidoso. No one there. And then I decided that maybe I'd have better luck in a bigger town, so I thought I'd keep heading west, go on to Las Cruces."

"Then why Cloudcroft?" Sarah asked. "It's sort of out of the way."

"If you take the main roads. But I came down the back way, along the 244. Prettier country, and it's actually more direct. And I figured it couldn't hurt to check out Cloudcroft, just to see. It was almost dark when I got here, so I thought I'd bunk in one of the cabins down off the highway. But I guess I must have been looking in just the right direction, because I thought I saw a light on top of the hill, coming down through the trees. I figured I'd better go check it out, even if it turned out to be nothing. Luckily, I'd heard of the Lodge, so I knew there was a hotel up the hill, even though I've never stayed here." He chuckled, and drank some more of his wine. "Too rich for my blood."

Something about those words helped to ease a bit of the tension in Sarah's neck and shoulders. He sounded so refreshingly normal, despite his model looks. Yes, the hotel would've been a little pricey for a lot of people, and if he was from Roswell, Cam probably wouldn't have seen the need to stay overnight anyway. The town was close enough to Cloudcroft that you could day-trip it.

"Me, too," she said. "I'm just here because...."

He lifted an inquiring eyebrow at her. "You wanted to see how the other half lives?"

She smiled. "Not exactly. I actually worked here. So did my father—he's...I mean, he was the chef."

The light seemed to go out of Cam's dark eyes. "I'm sorry."

"It's all right." Empty words. Of course it wasn't all right...it could never be all right... but that was the sort of thing you were supposed to say. "We've both lost people...haven't we?"

A nod. He glanced away from her, at the flames in the hearth as they flickered and danced. "I mostly try not to think about it."

Sarah couldn't argue with that. Every day she tried her best to do the same thing, to act as though the world wasn't gone. Well, that wasn't exactly true. The world itself was still here—the buildings and the trees and the animals. Only the people had disappeared, gone to gray dust.

"Anyway," she went on, "do you think there's a real possibility of people being in Las Cruces?"

Cam swallowed some more wine before he put his wine glass back down on the table. "I don't know. It only seemed like the most logical place to look." One hand rubbed at the stubble on his chin, absently, his thoughts clearly very far away.

Don't stare, she thought. It was hard not to, though. After so much time alone, just hearing the sound of another person's voice was enough to upset her fragile composure. Having the source of that voice be possibly the best-looking person she'd ever met...well, his looks made it all that much harder.

All right, if she was going to be completely objective, he wasn't perfect-perfect. His nose was long, and his lips on the thin side. Even so, the combination of his features still worked out to something pretty spectacular.

"I haven't heard anything from over there," she said. She reached for her wine but didn't drink, instead held the bowl of the glass cupped in her palms.

"'Heard'?" Cam repeated. "What do you mean?"

"I have a ham radio setup," Sarah explained, then quickly amended, "That is, it belonged to a friend of the family. He taught me how to use it. I've been scanning for weeks and haven't heard a damn thing. Except…."

His gaze sharpened. Those dark eyes suddenly seemed very piercing. "Except what?"

"At the beginning…or close to the beginning. Maybe the end of the beginning. Anyway, after everyone was gone, but while the power was still on, I was trying to figure out what to do, and I remembered Kyle's radio. So I went to his place and started running through the bands, hoping I could find something. I thought I heard a man's voice really briefly, but I lost the signal. I couldn't even make out anything of what he said. Maybe something about a lab, but even that's just a guess."

"A lab," Cam repeated, his tone musing. This time his gaze tracked toward the French doors, although of course you couldn't see anything of the grounds outside. Just utter pitch black, as though the resort was suspended in the center of an obsidian globe. "Like at Sandia?"

"In Albuquerque?"

"Yes." He retrieved his wine glass, drank a little more, put it back down. "They had a lot of labs there. Defense, classified stuff. Maybe someone at Sandia figured out a way to survive the Heat."

"'The Heat'?" Sarah hated to ask so many questions, but it was obvious she'd missed a lot, isolated up here as she'd been. "That's what it was called?"

"Well, it wasn't official or anything. It probably ran through the population more quickly here because you were so isolated, and there weren't many of you to begin with. Out in the rest of the world, it took a little longer. Enough for the disease to get a nickname that was passed around before everything went dead."

She supposed she couldn't argue with that. As to which scenario was worse, she couldn't really say. Up here in Cloudcroft, it seemed as if the whole thing was over and done with in the space of a day. Out in the world...apparently the apocalypse had lasted a bit longer than that.

"Anyway," Cam continued, "you'd think if anyone had figured out how to survive the disease, it would have been someone at a government installation, or at the CDC or someplace like that. So it makes sense that the person you'd heard speaking might have said something about a lab."

"I guess." Sarah didn't want to sound quite so dubious, but one syllable wasn't much to go on. If only that one brief burst had lasted longer than a second or two. But it hadn't, and no matter how she tried, she couldn't seem to lock on to that same channel again. "Albuquerque's a long ways away."

He nodded. "True, but it's not like there aren't plenty of cars just lying around for the taking."

"So you drove here?" Even as she asked the question, she had to wonder. If he had a car, then why the heavy rucksack?

"Part of the way. Then my truck ran out of gas. I guess I could've taken one of the cars abandoned on the road—sometimes right in the middle of the road—but something about that felt strange. The dust, you know?"

Oh, how she knew. She'd spent days cleaning the residue of the hotel's guests off the floor, off the beds. Never mind that no one would ever sleep in those beds again. It still seemed disrespectful to just leave the dust where it had fallen. Once, that dust had been people.

"I get it," she said. "Besides, the weather's been pretty nice lately."

"True. I think it helped to walk, actually. Gave me a chance to clear my head, come to grips with what was going on."

Sarah understood that sentiment as well. Some days, it seemed as if her walks in the woods were the only thing that kept her from going completely crazy. She hadn't wanted to contemplate what she'd do when the snows of winter closed in, if not trapping her in the hotel, then at the very least making it much more difficult to get out and about.

Cam yawned then, and sent her an apologetic glance. "Sorry. I'm up at dawn most of the time, and I guess it's catching up with me."

"That's all right." She hesitated. The situation was already strange enough, but it would be far stranger to have him stay here at the Lodge with her. But what else was she supposed to do…send him off to sleep at a cabin that hadn't been cleaned out, a house that still had its former inhabitants' dust lying on the floor? The hotel was nothing except empty rooms, all of them as clean as she could make them. Not the Governor's Suite, since she'd taken that one for her own, but there were several parlor suites with king beds that should suit Cam just fine. "Let me get you a key for one of the rooms. I have heat for cooking, but there's no running water, so—"

He shot her a startled glance. "Are you sure? I could find something else in town."

"No, it's all right. We survivors should stick together, right?" He still looked uncertain, so she added, smiling so he'd know it was a joke, "As long as you're not a serial killer or something."

A slow grin spread over his face. "No, I'm not a serial killer."

About all she could do was hope he was telling her the truth.

Chapter Three

KAMAL STRETCHED OUT ON THE BED AND STARED up at the ceiling, now faintly illuminated by the glow from the candle on his bedside table. Sarah had bidden him a good night and retired to her own suite, concealed behind a set of glass doors with heavy drapes that hid everything within. The exchange had been rather awkward, as though she understood all too well how odd it was for her to invite a stranger to sleep under her roof, even while acknowledging that it was probably better for them to remain together.

Well, it was a very large roof. And although the suite he now occupied was on the ground floor, the same as hers, it was at the opposite

end of the corridor, with windows that overlooked the hotel's extensive grounds. His djinn-
sharp eyes could make out the shape of a
gazebo, and an empty swimming pool beyond
that; scaffolding around the pool suggested it
had been undergoing construction at the time
the Heat swept through the world. Just as well;
without electricity, Sarah would have had a
difficult time draining it, a task that would have
had to be done before the winter freeze set in.

All in all, he was quite pleased with how
things had worked out so far. She had seemed
wary at first, but more curious than anything
else. Kamal could sense how relieved she had
been to speak to another human being...or at
least, someone she thought was a human being.

Good thing that he had studied these
mortals, had done his best to learn how to
mimic their speech patterns and idioms. He did
not think Sarah had noticed anything out of the
ordinary about his person; he'd made sure to
wear clothing that wouldn't attract notice, jeans
and a T-shirt and hoodie, and a canvas jacket
over that. Hiking boots, and a rucksack he'd
found in an outdoor store in Las Cruces. Of
course he hadn't gone anywhere near Roswell;
that entire story was pure fiction. He'd needed

something plausible to tell her, something that made him sound like a survivor from close enough by, if not a true neighbor. Just enough that she wouldn't find anything too strange, too alien about him.

Clearly she hadn't, or he wouldn't be lying here on this comfortable bed. It would have been even more pleasant if he could have shared it with her, but that, he knew, was expecting far too much too soon. He'd noted the obvious signs of attraction in her—quick, sidelong glances, a casual moistening of her lips, the way she smoothed her hair when she thought he wasn't looking—so he knew that their joining wasn't an impossibility. Far from it. All things in their own time, however.

Time…well, he'd have to see how much time all this would actually require. Sarah's comment about the water might have discomfited a mortal, but since Kamal was a water elemental, such minor inconveniences were no trouble for him. He'd thanked her for the pitcher of water she'd given him, saying there should be enough to have a glass to drink with some left over for washing-up, but he had no intention of using it for that purpose. All he had to do was go into the bathroom and lay a hand on the faucet, and the water would come gushing out. It wasn't even as though he had to conjure the water itself, for it lay in its holding tank beneath the hotel, simply waiting to be used.

A small talent, but still one he would have to conceal from Sarah. For now, anyway.

He'd enjoyed speaking with her, though, listening to the sound of her voice, low but soft, pleasant enough that he guessed he would not easily tire of it. And the way the firelight had glimmered in her big eyes, almost green in its golden glow, even though he knew her eyes were really blue. So lovely, even in the plain long-sleeved T-shirt she wore and her faded jeans.

Just the memory of her long, slim legs in those jeans, and the way her T-shirt had clung to her curves, was enough to make his blood run a little hotter. He told his body it would have to wait a while longer. She was friendly, but skittish nonetheless for all that. If he pushed himself on her too soon, he could ruin everything.

In the meantime, it was best to will himself to sleep, and know he would be able to spend more time with her tomorrow.

❄

Although she was physically tired—just as she was nearly every day, after managing all the minutiae of a life without electricity or running water—Sarah couldn't quite summon the calm she needed to fall asleep. It didn't help that the room was fairly cold, either; the bed was piled with extra blankets, but they could only do so much. The same with the fireplace in the sitting area of the suite. Thank God it was actually functional, but the small firebox didn't give off as much heat as she would have liked. Enough to take the edge off, and that was about it. The room came equipped with a portable heater to supplement the fireplace, but without electricity, the heater's only use was as an oversized doorstop. More than once, Sarah had wondered whether she should move her base of operations to someplace a little more convenient. Just down the street were several houses she'd always admired, new and large and well-maintained, built chalet-style into the side of the hill.

And yet she'd stayed, stubbornly clinging to this spot, even though she knew her father was long gone, that he wouldn't come walking back up the hill one day, full of stories about everything he'd survived since the world-changing fever had run its way through the population. Deep down, she'd understood that no one was going to find her here.

Except, improbably, someone had. And not just any "someone," but a guy probably only a few years older than she, darkly good-looking, friendly. Talk about the universe deciding that maybe it had been just a little too harsh after all.

Which of course it had. You couldn't exactly compare the thrill of having an unexpected companion—no matter how attractive—show up on your doorstep to the unspeakable tragedy of all those countless millions lost.

No, probably billions. She'd been so isolated here that she still didn't have a clear idea of the enormity of this disaster, but two people alive in a place even as lightly populated as New Mexico was a pretty clear indicator that this disease had a mortality rate that made Ebola look like the chicken pox.

Where had it even come from? She'd wondered about that a good bit, thinking maybe the disease was something that had escaped from a lab. Something right out of a science fiction novel, or a horror movie. No zombies here, though. Just dust, and emptiness.

She rolled over. On the nightstand was a small vanilla-scented votive candle in a glass holder; she couldn't bear to be alone in utter darkness these days, and always had to have a candle burning once the sun went down. At some point, she supposed, she'd run out of candles, although that day was a good ways off. Cloudcroft was small, but it had its own candle store, and there had also been some candles in the Family Dollar. She was working her way through those ones first, saving the good candles for later on, when she'd need them to combat the dark, dull days of winter and early spring.

If she stayed here. Maybe it would be better for her and Cameron to take the sturdiest vehicle they could find here in town, siphon as much gas they could carry—she'd discovered a bunch of gas cans in the maintenance shed, so transporting fuel wouldn't be a problem—and then head out, first for Las Cruces, and then up to Albuquerque. Surely there must still be people in Albuquerque, even if she hadn't been able to contact them on the radio. She refused to believe that the entire state was empty except for her and Cameron. There had to be survivors.

Somewhere.

Of course, all these plans were predicated on the assumption that the two of them would continue to get along, would decide to work together. For all she knew, a day or two in her presence would be enough to induce boredom, and Cam would want to move on. God knows it wouldn't be the first time.

All right, Seth hadn't exactly dumped her out of boredom. He'd wanted to get out of here, wanted her to move to Albuquerque with him so they'd both have a better chance of achieving something. Anything that wasn't waiting tables, or being a front desk clerk at a hotel. But she wouldn't leave, and he ended up going without her. She'd cried a little, and had some beers with friends, all of whom told her that Seth was a selfish jerk and that she could do better. She wanted to believe that.

But…what if *she* was the selfish jerk? What if she'd clung to her responsibility to her father because she didn't want to acknowledge that she was kind of scared shitless to try to make something of herself in the wide world beyond Cloudcroft?

Possibly. Not that it mattered now.

Anyway, she was getting ahead of herself.

She needed to wait and see how things worked out with Cameron. God knows he was easy on the eyes, but what if he turned out to be less than ideal? Maybe he would be lazy, and expect her to wait on him hand and foot. All right, that didn't sound like someone who'd just walked sixty miles on mountain roads to get here, but you just never knew for sure, did you? Or maybe he was a slob, or someone who wanted to spend all day talking about baseball scores.

Or maybe he'd try to get physical. There was a real conundrum, because she had to admit to herself that she didn't think she'd mind too much if he did. She knew basically nothing about him, but she did know she reacted to him on a visceral level, was drawn to those smoldering dark eyes, that lean, muscular build. All right, she couldn't really say his eyes smoldered, exactly, but they were so very dark and deep, fringed with amazing lashes. And that silky dark hair. If asked, she probably would have said she really wasn't into guys with long hair, that it seemed kind of feminine to her, but there was absolutely nothing feminine about Cameron.

Right then, she wasn't sure which would be

worse—if he got physical before she wanted him to, or if he never did.

What if he was gay? He didn't seem gay to her, but she'd be the first to admit that her gaydar wasn't exactly well calibrated. That would be a fine irony, though...to have the handsomest guy to survive the apocalypse right here in her lap, so to speak, and he wouldn't care at all about her lap because he'd really been hoping the survivor he found would turn out to be Sean, not Sarah.

All right, now would be a really good time to stop torturing yourself, she thought, and rolled over again, this time onto her back.

But she still couldn't quite get her mind to shut up. It was as though Cameron's presence had flicked over a switch, made her thoughts race, chasing one after the other. His story sounded plausible enough, and yet....

More than two months had passed since the world changed. Yes, he'd told her how he'd roamed the streets of Roswell and the farms and ranches outside the city, looking for any survivors, but would that kind of endeavor really take two whole months? She had to admit she wasn't as familiar with Roswell as she would have liked—she'd gone there off and or, one time with a bunch of friends to giggle at the UFO Museum and the kitschy shops that catered to the paranormal crowd, another time just passing through on her way to Carlsbad Caverns—but she didn't have a good grasp on how big the town really was, how many residential streets Cameron might have had to traverse. Just making a similar inspection of Cloudcroft had taken her a few days, and the tiny hamlet had fewer than a thousand permanent residents.

Anyway, what reason would he have to lie? Maybe he'd spent a few weeks just trying to get a handle on what had happened, steeling himself to face a changed reality. If that was the case, then he was probably in a better place than she. Sarah knew she should have left Cloudcroft weeks or even months ago, tried to find survivors in the wide world. But she hadn't, staying here out of fear, or vain hope, or maybe good old plain inertia.

Well, now she didn't have to go looking. She had someone here with her now, and things would never be the same.

Chapter Four

THE HOTEL FELT COMPLETELY EMPTY, SILENT, dead. And yet Kamal knew better, because he sensed the faint tingle at the back of his neck that told him a human was nearby. Not in the room down the hall—a quick glance let him know the door stood open, revealing a sort of sitting area with a desk and an armchair. A fire burned low in a hearth that was nearly out of his field of vision.

So Sarah had been there recently. He closed the door to his borrowed hotel room behind him and made his way out to the lobby. The fireplace here was not entirely cold, either; the coals from last night's fire smoldered quietly, ready to be brought to life once again. A pile of logs sat on the floor next to the hearth, so he added several to the coals, using a pair of enormous tongs to arrange them with care, so they might get the oxygen they needed to burn efficiently.

A rustle off to one side made him look up. Sarah stood there, dressed in jeans and a sweater. In each hand, she held a white-glazed mug. Steam curled up from those mugs, along with the rich smell of fresh-brewed coffee.

"I thought you might like some," she said, extending one of the mugs toward him.

"Thank you," he replied, and moved closer so he might take the coffee from her. On purpose, he had his fingers brush against hers, just to see how she would react. Color flamed in the fair skin of her cheeks, but she didn't flinch or try to move away from him.

Good.

"I hope you don't mind that I tended the fire," he went on, hoping his casual tone would defuse some of the tension in the room. A welcome kind of tension, to be sure, but he didn't want to put her too much on edge. He needed her to become relaxed around him, to become used to the reality of his presence.

"No, I don't mind. I meant to get to it, but then I thought I'd better get the coffee going."

"Yes, I remember you saying you had propane here."

"For now." A lift of the shoulders, an offhand gesture that didn't fool him for a second. "I try to be careful with it. Luckily, the tanks were filled just a day or so before…well, before. So I don't think too much of it got used up. It's hard to tell for sure, though."

"I can check," he offered, and her well-arched brows lifted in surprise.

"You can? I suppose I should know how to do it, but my father always took care of that sort of thing at the house—"

"Yes. I used to do some work on a ranch outside Roswell. They showed me how. I'll just need some hot water, though."

She smiled then, clearly relieved to have someone around to help with such mundane issues. "That I have, since I just boiled water for coffee. Let me go get the kettle."

"Sure." He got the impression that she wanted him to remain where he was, so he stayed standing in front of the fireplace, sipping at the hot coffee, as she disappeared through the bar and on into the hotel dining room. The kitchen must be located someplace beyond that.

The coffee was good, strong and rich. He wondered if she was using the stores left behind here at the Lodge, or whether this was something she'd gotten in town. Not that it mattered one way or another.

As for the trick with the propane—unlike many of his kind, who might deign to sample human cuisine, or listen to the music created by mortals, or visit one of their art galleries, but otherwise showed little interest in human affairs—Kamal had studied many facets of human life, especially the kind of life led by the people in this part of the country, the place that had once been New Mexico. He had known from early on who he wanted to be his Chosen, and so he had determined to immerse himself in the world she knew. Her future might be utterly changed from what she had once expected, and yet he hoped he could offer her a little familiarity.

Sarah returned, a stainless-steel kettle in one hand. "The tanks are out here."

He followed her through a set of French doors into the gardens. Now all the grass was yellow, faded into winter's dormancy. Frost glittered on that grass, and he saw Sarah shiver. The cold couldn't affect him as it did her, but he made a show of blowing on his hands as he walked, so she wouldn't comment on his lack of reaction to the near-freezing temperatures.

They went past the gazebo and the now perpetually under construction swimming pool. Kamal saw that Sarah was headed toward a long, low building half hidden behind a rise. "The maintenance shed," she explained, even though the structure seemed a good deal larger than the average shed.

Behind that building were two large white tanks. "Which one?" he asked.

"The one closer to us. It's the primary tank. I think it's supposed to get switched over when it's empty, but I honestly don't know if that's something that happens automatically, or whether we have to come out and do something about it."

Her expression was troubled, although Kamal couldn't be sure whether that concern was based on her lack of knowledge about the process, or merely worry that they might be very close to using up the first tank. "Well, let's see if it's anything we need to worry about in the near future," he told her. "After that, we'll worry about how we're supposed to switch the tanks." Her face brightened a little, and he went on, "Pour the hot water down the side of the tank. After that, I'll feel the metal. It'll be warmer in the part that's empty. The spot where it changes will tell us how much is left."

"Wow," she said, looking impressed. "It's really that simple?"

"Usually. Give it a try."

She lifted the kettle and poured a liberal amount of water onto the tank. The liquid steamed in the cold air, and Kamal hoped the ambient temperature, which appeared to be hovering a few degrees above freezing, wouldn't alter the results too much. He felt the metal, slowly sliding his hand down the surface of the tank.

There. Fairly high up, too, which meant the tank was a little more than three-quarters full. He didn't know exactly how much propane such mundane activities as using the stove actually consumed, but since they weren't utilizing the hot water heaters at the moment, he guessed it should go a long way. Long enough, at any rate. It wasn't as if the fuel needed to last through the winter.

Because as much as he would have liked to

linger here with Sarah for as long as proved necessary, Kamal knew he didn't have forever. A few weeks earlier, not too long after the day that used to be Thanksgiving when there were still those alive to celebrate it, he'd been called to speak to Zahrias al-Harith, the leader of the djinn community in Taos.

"I hope you don't plan for this little experiment of yours to go on indefinitely," Zahrias had said with a scowl. "Your games are not something the elders will smile upon."

"Oh, not indefinitely," Kamal replied. "Just long enough for me to be sure."

"The other djinn here did not need anything close to that length of time in order to be 'sure.'"

Kamal could only lift his shoulders. What the other djinn did or did not do when it came to their Chosen was of little concern to him. If they wanted to be reckless with their futures, so be it. He did not intend to make that same mistake.

"You have until the turn of the year, as the mortals reckoned it," Zahrias told him. "No more. If you are not among us by then, I cannot swear to the safety of your Chosen, for you know it was never intended for you to live apart from the rest of us."

"I understand," Kamal had said, and left Taos without feeling unduly burdened by the deadline Zahrias had imposed. Return to Taos with Sarah Wright by the turn of the year? That still gave him several weeks. Plenty of time.

If it required even that long. He did not wish to have to hide his water use from Sarah forever. Perhaps he would need to come up with some kind of plausible explanation for why they suddenly had running water at the Lodge. It did not seem as though she was all that technically inclined, and so he could probably offer some sort of jury-rigged device to satisfy her curiosity without providing too many details.

"We have a decent amount of propane," he said, and while she didn't exactly sag with relief, she did appear a little less tense. "More than three-quarters of the tank seems to be left, and since I have to think that these tanks probably lasted at least a week between refills, it should be enough for a good long while. It's not as if the hotel is full of guests."

The half smile that had touched her full mouth faded abruptly. "No," she said, "that it definitely isn't. Anyway, let's get inside. It's freezing."

He wouldn't argue with that. It wasn't that he couldn't tell how cold it was, only that the temperature had no real effect on him.

They traipsed back across the grounds, into the welcome warmth of the lobby. Sarah shut the door, locking it behind them.

After that was done, she looked back up at him. "Well, now that it's safe to cook…how about some biscuits and eggs?"

Cameron seemed to appreciate the breakfast she made for him—he ate every bit of the scrambled eggs, and had two biscuits, along with another cup of coffee. Thank God for the chickens, and the aplomb that allowed them to keep on laying serenely week after week, apocalypse or no. At first Sarah had thought of trying to move the chickens up to the hotel, maybe keeping them in the maintenance shed or one of the other outbuildings, but then she'd decided to let them stay where they were. They seemed content enough in their covered coops, although she still worried about what to do with them when the truly cold weather came.

She didn't have eggs all the time, mainly because she didn't have a good way of storing them without refrigeration, but she'd gathered a half-dozen the day before as she made her rounds through the town. The best way she'd discovered to keep the eggs cool was to put them in a basket she hung from the eaves of the hotel; that way, she didn't have to worry about any animals getting to them. She supposed a bear wouldn't have any trouble reaching the basket, although maybe the bears were already hibernating. So far this winter had been unnaturally mild, but she didn't know if the warmer-than-average temperatures would affect when the animals went into their winter sleep or not. Better to be safe.

Anyway, she had to admit it felt good on a visceral level to watch Cam eat the food she'd prepared for him with a healthy appetite. And he didn't complain about the lack of butter for his biscuits, or milk for his coffee. True, there was a decent supply of nondairy creamer in the pantry here, but she'd rather go without than put all those chemicals in her coffee. And although she'd put out a little basket of the nondairy containers, he didn't seem inclined to use any of them, either.

So there was something the two of them had in common. Such a little thing, and yet it made her feel slightly more relaxed about his presence here.

"That was great," he said, pushing his empty plate away from him. "Where do you keep the chickens? Somewhere on the hotel grounds?"

"No," she replied, then picked up both their dishes and set them on the counter next to the sink. Gone were the days when she could have simply turned on the tap to clean up, but later on she'd fill a bucket with water from the well and bring it in so she could wash their plates and forks and coffee mugs. "I didn't really have a good place to put them, unless I wanted to do some serious remodeling. Besides, I was worried that moving the chickens might upset them, keep them from laying. So I just go around and gather what I need, then bring it back here."

"And the water?"

"The hotel has its own well. But I have to pump it manually, which is why we're on rations."

To her surprise, Cameron smiled at her comment. "I might be able to help with that. Do you have any solar panels around here?"

"There are some here at the hotel, and there are houses around town that have them if you don't want to mess with what's already in place. Why? Are you a solar panel engineer or something?"

"No, but I've worked with them a bit. I could probably figure out a way to get some hooked up to the well's pump so we'd have running water. We'd have to be sparing with it, but it would be better than having to haul it manually from the well. And since the propane supply looks good, that means you'd have hot water again."

The mere thought of a hot shower, after all these weeks of tepid baths, was enough to send a shiver of anticipation through Sarah. Maybe some people would have taken offense at the way Cameron had casually begun to take over, but right then she didn't care. Having to go it alone these past two months had been hard. Right then, she was glad to have someone willing to shoulder some of the burden.

"Right down the street are some fancy vacation houses with solar setups," she said. "Do you want to take a look?"

"Sounds like a plan."

This time, they both paused to pull on their jackets before heading outside. Sarah led Cameron to the maintenance shed, where the golf cart she used to get around was plugged in, ready to go. Its charge wouldn't last as long when hauling Cam's weight as well as hers, but they didn't have all that far to travel.

"This way, I wouldn't waste any gas," she explained as she piloted the cart out of the shed and down one of the little access trails on the property. "There are abandoned cars all over town, and a gas station, but this just seemed simpler for getting around."

"Makes sense." He was quiet for a moment, watching the hotel's grounds give way to the narrow residential streets that bordered the property. "It's hard to pump gas without electricity. I know there's some kind of manual override to bypass the electrical systems at gas stations, but I have no idea how that works."

Unlike propane tanks and solar panels, apparently. Sarah didn't comment, though. She was just glad that he had a solution to their water problem.

Unlike her. For a moment, she felt a stir of irritation with herself, then realized she needed to let it go. She'd done okay these past few months. It wasn't as though she could really expect herself to turn into some kind of technical genius just because the apocalypse had rolled around and made such skills more important than ever.

They came to one of the houses she had in mind, and she eased the cart down the steep driveway, hoping the little vehicle would have enough juice to get back up once they were done. She'd already foraged in this house, but had done so on foot because it was close enough to the hotel that it wasn't any real burden to take back a few bags of supplies. Solar panels, on the other hand, were a heck of a lot bulkier.

"They have some panels mounted on the roof," she explained as Cam got out of the cart and began looking around. "But there's also an array on the hillside right below the house."

"Show me," he said, with such a note of command in his voice that she couldn't help raising an eyebrow. However, she told herself that he was probably just eager to see the solar panels, figure out if they would work.

"This way," she replied, and headed toward the north side of the property so they could skirt the house itself and come out in the steep "yard"—really, not much more than patchy bare dirt with a few seedling pines to break up the monotony—to the west.

Cam strode past her once he caught sight of the solar panels, a modest array of about ten of them, all two feet by three feet. Luckily, they weren't so big that they wouldn't fit in the back of the golf cart.

Without speaking, he started inspecting the undersides of the panels, the conduit that must connect them to the house's electrical grid. After a long moment, he seemed to nod to himself, then flipped open a panel at the back and began disconnecting the wires he found there.

"Do you think they'll work?" she asked.

A nod, but Cameron didn't glance up from his task. "I think so. Like I said, they won't give us a lot of power, but it's not as if we're going to be running the air conditioning units or something like that. The well doesn't need to draw a lot of energy."

"What about the refrigerator?"

"I don't know. We'll have to see."

She experienced a small stab of disappointment at his reply, but tried to tell herself that having running water was more important than refrigeration. Because it was so cold now, she could keep perishables outside if she was worried about their freshness. Even during the day, high temperatures were barely hitting forty. Besides, she'd already lost the really important stuff—the meat and cheese and dairy —in the days right after the power failed. She'd had to grimly load all of it into plastic garbage bags, drive it out into the forest, and dump everything. Now the only thing she really had to worry about refrigerating was the eggs.

Cameron's fingers moved on the mounts that held the solar panels to their housings. Sarah couldn't tell exactly what he was doing, but a minute or so later, he had one of them free. "Can you take this?" he asked. "It's not too heavy."

She wanted to tell him that she was perfectly capable of carrying heavy objects, but getting snarky would serve no purpose. Instead, she nodded and took the solar panel from him, then hauled it across the yard and back up to where the electric cart waited. The panel did fit in the back…barely. By the time she was done, Cameron had a second panel loose. Since they seemed to have agreed upon a system, she lifted it in silence and again took it to the cart as her companion kept working. When he had the third panel freed, however, he picked it up himself and met her as she was coming back from the cart.

"This should be enough for now," he said. "No point in ripping up the whole yard if I can't get any of this to work."

"All right." Actually, that sounded like a great idea. Although no one could ever have accused her of being out of shape, carrying the heavy panels uphill in rough terrain wasn't exactly a picnic. Better to find out whether Cam's plan was at all practical before she spent all morning wearing herself out.

They got in the cart and went back to the hotel, the little vehicle puttering along, clearly not happy about the extra burdens of the solar panels, not to mention a well-muscled six-foot-two man. Or maybe six foot three, Sarah mused as she drove around to the back of the hotel, getting them as close as the paths would allow to the site of the well. Cameron might not be a full foot taller than she, but since she was only five foot four, she thought he was pretty damn close to that.

He picked up all the panels at once without showing any real sign of strain. So…strong, too. Tall, dark, and handsome.

Oh, boy.

Without speaking, she followed him to the well. It really didn't look like all that much—a round metal manhole, a few oddly shaped metal pipes sticking out of the ground a few feet away.

"I'll just lay the panels flat for now," Cameron said, kneeling on the cold, hard-packed earth as he pried up the well cover. "That won't work in the long run—they need to be up off the ground. But again, there's no point in building a frame for them if I can't get them to play nice with the wiring in the well's pump." He set the heavy metal lid off to one side, then stuck his head inside the opening.

"Do you see anything?" Sarah asked. She'd never actually lifted the well's lid, worrying that if she started mucking around inside, she might really screw up something, or possibly contaminate the water. The manual pump was located some distance away, over by the main-tenance shed, and so didn't require her to work with the well itself. Anyway, with no electricity, there hadn't been much point in messing with the well.

"I see the pump. And I see the wiring harness." He pulled his head out of the dark hole in the ground, pushing back his overlong hair. It wasn't quite long enough to tie back into a ponytail, so Sarah could see why it might get in the way.

For some reason, though, all she really wanted was to run her hands through that hair. Trying to blink that image out of her mind, she said, "And that means...?"

"It means I need some tools." He got to his feet and brushed at the dirty knees of his jeans.

"There are tools in the maintenance shed. I can go get them—"

"No, it's better if I can just go get what I need. This might take a while, so there's no point in you standing around out here in the cold."

"I don't mind."

"But I do." He flashed her a quick grin, the kind of smile that could melt kneecaps at fifty paces. "Don't worry—I'll yell if I need you."

"All right," she said reluctantly. "If you need anything—"

"I'll call."

"Okay." She offered him a smile of her own, although she doubted hers was quite as brilliant as the grin he'd given her just a moment earlier. As she turned to go back into the hotel, she saw him head off toward the maintenance shed, his head high, confident.

Sarah supposed she'd see soon enough whether that confidence was at all misplaced.

Chapter Five

Of course he wasn't really going to hook up the solar panels to the wiring harness. Kamal just had to make it look as if he had. It was his djinn powers that would actually set the water flowing again on the property.

Since he'd made sure that Sarah wouldn't look at his work too closely, he pulled some wires up to the solar panels, then wrapped them with black electrical tape. Nothing that would fool an expert, or even a halfway knowledgeable hobbyist, but good enough. As he worked, the skies overhead began to lower, growing darker, heavier. Because his element was water, he could sense the moisture in those clouds, the gathering storm. The season might have been mild so far, but he was certain that snow was on its way.

Well, let it snow. He and Sarah had done their exploring for the day, and could retreat inside where it was warm and safe. That suited him well enough, because then he could spend more time in close proximity to her. He was pleased by the way she'd worked with him this morning, carrying the heavy loads of those solar panels with not one word of complaint. Then again, after the past few months, she'd probably gotten used to doing what she needed to in order to survive.

He returned the tools to the maintenance shed, then began to walk back toward the hotel. As he went, the first fat flakes of snow began to fall, so light and insubstantial it hardly seemed they could be formed of water, must instead be drifting down from some celestial feather bed. They'd barely dusted his hair and shoulders before he was safely inside in the relative warmth of the Lodge's kitchen. A faint trace of heat remained from the breakfast Sarah had prepared earlier, although he knew the lobby must be more comfortable. He could smell the wood smoke from here.

Sarah was standing by the fireplace, a heavy

log in one hand. At his approach, she set it down and gave him an expectant glance. "How did it go?"

"Come see for yourself."

Her head tilted slightly to one side, but she didn't argue. In silence, she followed him into the kitchen. Her expression was skeptical—one eyebrow at a slight tilt, mouth not quite pursed.

Very well. He knew she had every reason to doubt him, but he also knew something she didn't.

He reached over to the faucet and turned the tap. Water began to pour out, filling the pitcher he'd set there in preparation for this moment.

Sarah's eyes widened, startlingly blue. "Oh, my God! You did it!" Clearly not skeptical now, she hurried over to the sink and put a finger under the tap, as though she still had to feel the water for herself to believe that it really was flowing, wasn't just a product of her imagination.

"Well, I don't know how much of a charge the panels are going to get this morning. It's started to snow. So it's probably better to play it safe." He shut off the tap before turning to face her.

She didn't appear too discomfited by his comment. "Still...you got it to work." Her gaze shifted, moving toward one of the windows in the far wall. Outside, the snow had continued to fall, still not thick enough to coat anything, although Kamal could tell the temperature was cold enough that the precipitation should stick. "That's more than I've been able to manage."

He did not wish to see her deprecate herself. After all, he hadn't managed any great technical feats of his own, had only made her believe that what he had done with his powers was the result of scientific knowledge rather than inborn talent. "You managed a lot," he said. On impulse, he reached out and took her hands in his. Her fingers felt small and cold, and he wrapped his hands around hers, hoping he could warm her— and also hoping that she wouldn't try to pull away. If she did, he wouldn't stop her, for he would take such a gesture as a signal she was not quite ready for any sort of physical contact, even something as innocuous as holding hands.

However, she didn't pull away. She stood there, her slender body quite still, as though she wasn't sure what she should do.

Encouraged, Kamal went on, "You've

survived here for two months, all on your own. You've kept yourself safe. That's a lot, even if you don't think it is."

Her eyes met his. Such a clear, beautiful color, like purest aquamarine. "No, I'm a coward. I should have left. I should have gone to look for other survivors—"

"There aren't any," he broke in. "I've looked, too. I've found no one except you."

She seemed to falter then, her gaze moving away from him to focus on the slow-falling snow outside the windows.

"And if you'd left," he continued, "I would have come here and found this place empty. If you'd gone down the hill into Tularosa or Alamogordo, if you'd continued to White Sands and on through the mountain passes into Las Cruces...I probably would never have met you."

A long pause. Her hands were warming within his grasp, coming to life. She looked up at him, mouth set. When she did speak, her voice was so low, even his djinn ears had to strain to hear her words.

"Would that have been so awful?"

"Yes," he said, knowing the word was no

more than the truth. "It would have been terrible."

This was the time. He bent, and touched his lips to hers. Gently—oh, so very gently, because he could tell that she was on the edge, might bolt if he was too forceful. But oh, how he had wanted to kiss her in that moment, her eyes wide and tragic, face pale but no less beautiful for all that.

And she accepted the kiss. She did not pull away, did not tear her hands from his and go running for the sanctuary of the suite she'd claimed as her own. She stood there, mouth warm and welcoming, and allowed him to taste her at last, to put his arms around her so he might pull her close.

They stood that way for a long moment, and then he did let her go so she could try to recover herself. She pushed her heavy brown hair away from her face and stood there in silence for a moment. At last she gave him a lopsided smile and said, "Wow, that was fast. I thought we'd at least make it two or three days before that sort of thing happened."

"Do you mind?" he asked, genuinely curious.

"Do I...?" She chuckled, although there was

something forced about the sound. "I'm not sure 'mind' is the right word. I mean, it's probably silly to get hung up on 'should' and 'would' when it's the end of the world, right?"

"Right," he echoed. "You just—you just looked so happy then, when the water came out of the tap. And then you looked sad, as though you thought you were somehow lesser because you hadn't been able to do that hack on your own. Don't put yourself down, Sarah. You don't deserve it."

One hand went up to play with the thin silver chain she had around her neck. It wasn't a cross she wore, which might have been expected, but a small, stylized version of the Zia sun symbol that had once adorned New Mexico's flag. A powerful sigil, with its four rays multiplied by four—the points of the compass, the stages of life, the seasons of the year, the times of day. He wondered why she had chosen it, rather than a more obvious symbol of faith.

"I guess," she said after a long pause. "Or at least, I'll try to tell myself that I shouldn't think that way. I suppose I'm shaking my head at the universe. Here the world's ended, and everything is awful, and then...and then suddenly

Mr. Perfect shows up on my doorstep. My borrowed doorstep, anyway."

"You think I'm Mr. Perfect?" Kamal asked, amused. He supposed that, to a mortal, a djinn would seem perfect...although he doubted his fellow elementals would ever assign such an adjective to him.

"Oh, God, that sounded terrible, didn't it?"

"I don't know about terrible," he responded, then reached out so he could take her hands and pull her close to him once more. "I kind of liked the sound of 'Mr. Perfect.'"

"Great. Now you have a swollen head."

He could have made an off-color joke in answer to that comment, but realized that would not have gone over terribly well. Yes, they had kissed, but they weren't quite at the point where they could bandy ribald words with one another. He settled for saying, "Not yet," before he bent and kissed her again.

Sarah didn't seem inclined to protest. She allowed him to hold her, to claim her mouth with his, and Kamal decided that was enough for now.

❄

Cam was acting so…normal, like they hadn't just shared a couple of fairly intense kisses. Then again, what was he supposed to do? Go down on one knee and declare his undying love for her? They barely knew one another.

No, he'd poured a glass of water for each of them, then led her out to the lobby, where they could sit by the fire and watch the snow float down gently, just beginning to cover the deck outside and the landscape beyond. This snow seemed more determined than the flurries she'd experienced so far this season, and she wasn't quite sure how she should feel about that. On the one hand, there was something very cozy about being here by the massive fireplace with its gleaming copper hood, knowing that you were warm and inside and away from the weather.

And not alone. She'd begun to think she would never see another human being, and then…

…and then along came Cameron. Besides being handsome and smart and resourceful, he really knew how to kiss. Strong, yet tender. Passionate without being overbearing. He smelled good, too, like wood smoke and pine trees and all the things she liked.

Even with all that, she wasn't sure she liked the idea of the snowfall. Something about it seemed so final, as though they'd lost their last chance to get off this mountain before winter really set in. Sarah had been fairly sure she had enough food to support her through those long, cold months, but with two of them here? She'd have to redo all her calculations, and hope to hell she could make everything stretch.

"Hey," Cameron said, and she startled, realizing that she'd been staring at the fire and frowning fiercely. "Are you all right?"

"Fine," she replied, an automatic response. "Just thinking about winter."

"You're worried?"

"A little."

"Don't be."

His arm went around her, pulled her close. There was something awfully comforting about having such a strong shoulder to lean her head on. That had been the worst of it—to grieve alone, to have to come to grips with such a change in the world with no one there to talk to, no one to comfort her during the dark, frightening nights, when the entire planet seemed to echo with its emptiness.

Now someone was here...an amazing some-one...and yet she was still worrying.

"I don't have to worry because now you're here to take care of me?"

"That's not what I said." He shifted on the couch so he could look down into her face. His dark eyes were intent, holding hers so fiercely, she didn't think she could glance away, even if she wanted to. "It's pretty clear that you're able to take care of yourself. I just think...well, it's usually easier if you don't have to shoulder the load all alone. That's all."

How could she argue with a comment like that, when she'd just been thinking basically the same thing a few minutes earlier? "You're right," she said. "And it's still early for the really heavy storms. Most of that seems to wait until after Christmas, even though we'll get some before then. Which is good. It doesn't feel like Christmas if it's not snowy outside."

Cameron was quiet for a moment, his gaze moving around the large room where they sat. "Did they decorate a lot for the holidays here?"

"Oh, yeah. Pine garlands on all the banis-ters, lights outside, a huge tree in the lobby." Sarah could feel herself smiling as she recalled the Lodge in all its holiday splendor. "It looked like something out of a Hallmark Christmas special or something."

Her companion nodded, although something seemed a little hesitant about the smile he wore, as if he didn't quite know what a Hallmark Christmas special actually was. Well, she couldn't give him too much grief over that. Hallmark tended to be kryptonite for guys.

"After the snow lets up, maybe we can do something about that," he said. "I mean, I know the solar panels I set up won't be enough to power a lot of exterior lights or anything, but we could go out and gather pine boughs for garlands, at least enough to decorate in here. Would you like that?"

Of course she would. Usually by now the decorations would have already been in place, but she really hadn't been thinking about Christmas. Survival had consumed most of her thoughts. "I'd love it," she replied. "God knows, the one thing we have plenty of here in Cloudcroft is pine trees."

"All right, it's a date." He brushed her hair away from her face and kissed her again, this time softly on the cheek. "We'll just have to see how long this storm lasts."

Chapter Six

As it turned out, the snow fell for most of the day. Kamal could tell Sarah was disappointed that she wouldn't be able to go out and start gathering supplies for the holiday garlands right away. However, she told him that they might as well go down to the basement and begin going through the decorations stored there.

"We won't need to put up everything," she explained as she led him down the cellar stairs, a Coleman lantern in one hand. "But if we go through it and stage what we need, then when we do have a chance to go out and cut the fresh boughs, we'll have a better idea of how much to get."

That sounded like a practical plan to him. Also, it was good to see her animated and happy, thinking ahead. Although the djinn did not celebrate Christmas, they did observe the winter solstice, and the world's return from the short, dark days of that season. It would be good to see the Lodge dressed up in its holiday garb.

As Sarah began to go through box after box of decorations, he reflected that she hadn't been joking when she said the hotel staff went all out with its holiday trim. It seemed there was enough stored down here in the basement to adorn every doorway in the hotel—which wasn't all that far off from the truth.

"We used to put little wreaths on all the doors," she explained as she pushed a box filled with the little faux-greenery rings out of the way. "People thought it was a nice touch. But I don't think there's much point in going that crazy."

"No, probably not," he agreed, relieved that he wouldn't be drafted to hang wreaths on every door in the place. "And for the front door, we'll have fresh pine."

"That's the plan. Luckily, I've helped put those together, so I know what to do. I'm still looking for the florist's wire, though. I know there are a couple of spools of it somewhere around here." Sarah settled back on her heels and surveyed the boxes scattered on the floor around them, as though she had X-ray vision and could see inside each and every container.

"I'm sure it'll turn up."

"I hope so. Otherwise, I'll have to see if I can dig up some in town. I don't think the Family Dollar would carry anything like that, but Mrs. Ortega used to make and sell wreaths during the holidays. There's probably some stored in her house." Up until that moment, Sarah had looked happy, animated, but her expression darkened then. No doubt she was thinking of how the aforementioned Mrs. Ortega would have no further need of florist's wire…or anything else, for that matter.

Because Kamal didn't want Sarah to dwell on such things, he said quickly, "I'm sure we'll come across it. What about that box?" He pointed to a large container that hadn't yet been opened.

"No, those are the Christmas tree decorations. We won't need those for a while." She still seemed subdued, leading him to remark,

"Well, at least not until closer to the holiday." He had to mentally count out the days. Six to go.

Sarah tilted her head at him. "Maybe it's not such a good idea. I mean, have you ever actually cut down a pine tree?"

"No," he said. "But it can't be that difficult."

"I don't know." A small pause, and then she added, "Doesn't it seem sort of wasteful? Back in the day I really didn't think about it—we're surrounded by trees here, after all—but why cut a tree's life short, just to hang sparkly things on it for a week or so?"

Kamal guessed that she was talking about more than simply trees. His tone gentle, he said, "Possibly, but trees die all the time. Bark beetles, lightning strikes...there's no guarantee they'll be around forever. So I wouldn't worry about it. If the time comes and you want a tree, then we'll get one. Okay?"

Still she seemed to hesitate. Then she gave a reluctant nod. "Okay."

Something else seemed to be bothering her. Was she regretting the kisses they'd shared? He couldn't think of a way to ask without sounding as though he was questioning their newfound intimacy as well, and so decided it was better not to say anything.

A few minutes passed as she sorted through the boxes, setting aside spools of ribbon in shades of red and gold, and pre-made miniature arrangements of silk and plastic flowers and leaves. A small sigh escaped her lips. "Are we stupid for doing this?"

"Doing what?"

She gestured toward the clutter of holiday decorations around her. "Getting all this out… pretending everything is normal. That snowstorm isn't going to last forever, but there'll be more to come. Maybe we should get down off this mountain while we still can."

"I don't think we need to decide that now," he said carefully. Of course there was no way he could tell her that they'd be gone by the first of the year. Or rather, he knew he would have to tell her the truth soon enough, but they still had time. For some reason, he found himself strangely reluctant to broach the subject. Insane as it sounded, he enjoyed interacting with her as if he was just another mortal. Would she treat him the same way once she found out that he wasn't quite human?

"Then when?" She pushed herself to her feet, brushed at the dusty knees of her jeans.

"The weather won't hold back just because we don't feel like making a decision right now."

Since she had stood up, Kamal rose as well. He went to her and took her hand. Noting some resistance in her touch, he decided he wouldn't pull her close to him. At least she hadn't attempted to snatch her hand out of his grasp. This way they were still touching, even if an actual embrace didn't seem like the correct thing to do at the moment.

"If it looks like we're going to get a truly bad storm…well, then we'll make sure we're ready to leave. Surely someone up here in Cloudcroft was equipped to plow the roads?"

Sarah gave a reluctant nod. "Jeff Hansen. He lives…lived…at the far end of town. Made some extra cash every winter by getting one of those plow attachments for his truck and using that to keep things clear."

"So we have a way of getting down the hill," Kamal said. "Even if the weather gets bad."

"I suppose so."

This time he did pull her close. She didn't protest when he bent and kissed her. In fact, she let go of his hand so she could put her arms around him and press herself against his body.

Even through the bulky sweater she wore, he could feel her breasts touching his chest, and a wave of desire passed over him, so intense that he had to force himself not to lift her from the floor, take her upstairs so he could make love to her right away. Somehow he managed to remain calm, even as he kissed her and held her, and breathed in the warm scent of her skin.

She stepped away at last, and offered him a shaky smile. "Did I look that needy?"

"I don't know about 'needy,'" he replied. "I just know that I wanted to kiss you."

"I wanted to kiss you, too." This was said almost shyly, as though she was surprised by her own ardor.

Kamal couldn't blame her for that. She'd spent the last few months merely existing, probably ignoring the needs of her body, at least for anything beyond eating and sleeping and staying warm. "Then let's go upstairs where it's not so dusty and damp, and I'll kiss you some more."

This time she laughed—a true laugh, with nothing forced about it. "Sounds like a plan."

❄

Sarah hadn't really expected to spend part of the apocalypse lying on a couch in the lobby of the Lodge and making out like she was still back in high school. But that was exactly what happened—as soon as they got back upstairs, Cameron led her out to the room where they'd sat and watched the snow, only this time he pushed her down onto the sofa, his body heavy and strong on top of hers, his mouth more insistent now. She responded in kind, wanting this.

Wanting him.

And when he slid his hands up under her sweater, bare skin against bare skin, she hadn't tried to stop him. No, not even when his fingers moved across her breast. She was wearing a bra, but she could still feel the warmth of his flesh through the thin fabric. Her nipples went hard, and he probably felt that, too. He didn't say anything, though, only removed his hand after a few caresses, as if he knew she wasn't quite ready to go any further than that.

Actually, though, she thought she might be. Pooled, throbbing heat between her legs made her realize how much she wanted him. However, she told herself she needed to be smart about this. For one thing, she hoped he had some condoms hidden in that rucksack of his, because no way was she going to bed with him if he didn't have protection. The apocalypse was bad enough without risking an unplanned pregnancy.

They both sat up. Sarah did her best to smooth her mussed hair, while Cam surreptitiously tugged at his jeans.

Probably hiding a raging boner in there, she thought with an inward grin. Or at least, she really hoped he was. That way, she'd know she had the same effect on him that he had on her.

"It's stopping," he said, and she raised an inquiring eyebrow. "The snow," he added, by way of explanation, as he pointed toward the French doors.

Sure enough, although the skies still looked gray and heavy, the white flakes falling from the clouds had dwindled to almost nothing. Sarah got up from the couch and went to the door, straightening her sweater and adjusting the bra underneath, which wasn't lying quite where she wanted it. She had to hope Cameron wasn't paying attention, was still looking at the view outside. The yard and the grounds beyond it had a fairly respectable coating of white now, the landscape blurred by what she calculated was around three or four inches of snow.

"Good," she said. "That's just enough to be pretty without getting in the way too much. But it'll be dark soon, so I think we have to forget about bough-gathering until tomorrow."

"That's fine. It's the kind of night that's better for staying in."

He spoke in a neutral tone, but Sarah still felt another rush of heat go through her at his words. The memory of the kisses they'd shared, his hand on her breast, was far too vivid. Her body wanted more. She'd never been the type to jump into bed with people, so she really couldn't explain her current behavior. Then she wanted to laugh at herself. "People"? Three boyfriends in total, and the first one had been the love of her sophomore year in high school. She hadn't slept with him, had told herself that she wasn't ready. She probably wasn't ready to sleep with Chris, the guy she dated when she was nineteen, either, but at that point, she'd decided it was stupid to hang on to her virginity as though it was something precious as diamonds. No deep-held religious convictions held her back, no desire to wait until she was married or anything like that. It was just…the timing hadn't seemed to work until then.

Chris ended up joining the Marines and moving away, and after him had come Seth. She'd thought she and Seth could make it work. He'd had bigger plans, though. Plans he'd hoped would include her, but she was too much of a chickenshit to leave everything she'd known behind.

Well, it was all gone anyway, so her cowardice hadn't served much purpose. Or rather, Cloudcroft was still here, but everything that had it made it the town she loved—her father and the people she worked with, Louise at the candle shop and Marybeth at the turquoise store, her friend Candy who waited tables at Conrad's—all that had disappeared as the Heat swept over the world.

Worried that Cameron might read too much into her long hesitation, she said, "Yes, it is a good night to stay in. And I saved some potatoes, so I'll make soup. Sound good?"

The smile he gave her then was warm, eager. "Sounds great."

Besides the potatoes, she had a couple of precious cans of cheddar cheese soup, some evaporated milk, and canned corn. Combined with some seasonings and a dash of Worcester-shire sauce, the ingredients made some surprisingly tasty potato cheese soup. They had biscuits, too, and a bottle of wine she'd liberated from the Noisy Water Winery a while back.

Cameron had busied himself as well, and stoked the fire in the hearth that separated the bar from the restaurant's dining room. Sarah hadn't touched it all the time she'd been living here alone, but he insisted, saying that she'd gone to a lot of effort to make their dinner, so they should sit down and eat it at one of the dining tables like civilized people.

As he opened the wine, he glanced over at the grand piano that sat on a little dais next to the hearth. "Do you play?"

"No," she replied. "I wish I did. It would have given me something to do with my time. Do you?"

"No," he said. "No money for piano lessons in my family."

Sarah could relate to that. Cam's confession only relaxed her more. They might have only known each other for a couple of days, but she could tell that their backgrounds were very similar. Working class, or maybe the bottom layer of the middle class, but certainly no pretensions to anything more than that. If he'd been some rich guy from Santa Fe, he would have intimidated her.

As it was...she just liked being with him.

They drank wine, and ate their soup and biscuits. Their conversation turned to what they might do with all this snow...see if any of the snowmobiles up at Jensen's rental place had gas in them...build a snow fort... revive the covered skating rink at the end of town. Anything but fret about how the snow might have cut them off from the outside world. How could you even worry about something that didn't exist anymore? Cameron coming here was a one in a million shot; Sarah doubted more refugees would be making their way up the steep highway to see if anyone was still alive in tiny Cloudcroft.

The fire was warm, the wine rich and deep. Maybe too heavy for the light meal, but she wasn't complaining. It wasn't as if she had to worry about driving. No, they would stay here, safe and warm. Or mostly warm. The fireplace in her room did okay, but the guest room where Cam was sleeping didn't have a fireplace. Overnight, as the temperatures dropped and the skies cleared, that room would only get colder and colder.

She didn't want him to get cold. She wanted....

Across the table, their eyes met. His were so deep and dark, with such heavy lashes, they didn't look real. Sarah wondered if he had some Italian or Greek or something similar in his background, despite his very Anglo-Saxon last name. He did seem almost too exotic to have come out of prosaic Roswell, New Mexico.

Neither of them spoke. For a long moment, they sat there in silence, and then Cameron got up from his chair and extended a hand to her. She hesitated, knowing what the gesture meant. If she reached out her hand to take his, then this evening would move forward to its inevitable conclusion. And if she refused, instead picked up her glass so she could drink the remainder of the wine within, she'd be telling him she wasn't ready, that he was rushing things.

Which would it be?

His eyes held hers. Steady, calm, but with a fire deep within. He would be hurt by her refusal, but she somehow knew that he wouldn't push her.

This was crazy. She hardly knew him. She

should pick up her wine, offer him a smile, act as if everything was normal.

It wasn't normal, though. Nothing would be normal again.

Sarah took a breath, and laid her hand in Cameron's.

Chapter Seven

Her fingers felt so fragile in his, so delicate. And yet he'd seen those same small hands carrying solar panels earlier, and later efficiently chopping their precious store of potatoes into neat cubes for their soup. Kamal knew Sarah was anything but fragile.

Still, he also knew he needed to be careful.

He'd intended to guide her back to his room, but where the hallway branched off, she shook her head and tugged him toward the wing where her suite was located. "I have a fireplace," she murmured.

Well, he couldn't argue with that. Although a chilly room wouldn't bother him, it would make her uncomfortable, and the last thing he wanted was for her to be uncomfortable. Besides, making love with a fire crackling in the background was always a desirable thing.

The suite was larger than he had first thought, with the bedroom and bathroom branching off to the right, and a little sitting area with a couch, desk, and television set to the left. No wonder Sarah had taken up residence here. The parlor room she'd given him to sleep in was certainly comfortable enough, but it couldn't compare to this suite.

Logs had already been laid in the hearth, so all he had to do was take a long match from the box sitting on the mantel and touch it to one of the kindling twigs to get the fire going. If his element had been fire rather than water, he wouldn't have needed the match at all—well, except that using djinn talents in such a way would immediately alert Sarah that her companion wasn't quite as human as he pretended to be.

They would have to have that conversation at some point, but for now, he only wanted to focus on her. On the silky hair that slipped over his hands as he cupped her face and kissed her again, on the smooth white sweetness of her flesh after he'd taken hold of her sweater and pulled it over her head. The bulky clothing she wore had done its best to conceal the graceful curves of her body, but there was no hiding them now. His fingers traced lightly over the swell of her breasts, and she pulled in a little startled gasp of a breath, although he noticed she did nothing to stop him, only moved closer so he could reach behind her and undo the hooks of her bra. Like the rest of her clothes, it was a utilitarian enough garment, plain white, no lace or anything to adorn it.

Not that her beautiful breasts needed anything to enhance them. They fell free, full and rounded, so delicious-looking that he could do nothing but bend his head and take one rosy-brown nipple into his mouth, delighting in its hardness beneath his tongue. She moaned, her fingers catching in his hair as she held him close.

It was good to stand here in front of the fire and taste her, but he thought they would both be more comfortable in the bed, only a few paces off to the right. He slipped his arms under her and lifted her, eliciting another gasp, followed by a delighted smile. With one hand he reached out and tugged down the sheets and blankets, then deposited her on the bed. Right then he wished very much he had already told her he was a djinn, for he could have simply snapped his fingers and made the rest of her clothes disappear.

Since he knew doing so wasn't feasible, instead he took one of the heavy boots she wore and unlaced it, then did the same with the other before tugging both of them off, along with her thick socks. Next came the jeans, although he left her panties in place for now. They, too, were plain white, but he found them enticing nonetheless, for he knew what they concealed.

"No fair," she said, wrapping her arms around herself, although Kamal didn't know whether she did so because she was cold, or because she was suddenly shy now that she was nearly naked while he remained fully clothed. "If I have to freeze, so do you."

"I can stir up the fire, if you like."

"You've already done that," she responded, giving him a wicked smile. "What I really want is you in this bed with me."

Ah, he could definitely indulge her in that request. As she stared up at him, he unzipped the hoodie he wore, then pulled off the T-shirt he had on beneath it, followed by his own boots and socks and jeans. "Better?" he asked.

"Oh, yes," she said, her gaze taking in his unclothed form. "Much better."

That was as good an invitation as any. He got into bed next to her, pulled her close so he could feel her naked breasts rubbing against him. A small sigh escaped her lips, and she reached down to touch him, to feel the hardness of his shaft beneath the cotton undergarments he still wore.

This time he was the one who sighed—no, to be fair, that was more of a gasp. He decided to let her know that turnabout was fair play, and took hold of the underpants she wore, pulling them down so he could reveal the small patch of dark hair between her legs, could slip his finger into her, feel how aroused she was, how wet and ready.

Right then, all he wanted was to bury himself in her, but he also knew it would be best to go about this slowly, to make every inch of her respond to him. He wanted to make sure that this experience with him would far surpass any she might have had with a mortal lover. Yes, he could tell she was not a virgin, but at the same time, he did not think she was one to have given her body freely. She had not yet experienced everything that the world of lovemaking had to offer.

His tongue moved over her breast again as he stroked her. Another moan, this one lower, more guttural. He could hear how her breathing began to speed up, how her heart began to pound harder.

Yes. She cried out, her body spasming around his fingers. Good. He was somewhat surprised by how quickly she had responded, but then, she had gone without for several months...at least. Although she had said nothing yet of her past lovers, Kamal had the impression that she was alone when the Heat descended.

Some men might have left off there, but he was not yet done. He grazed kisses all down her flat stomach, pausing so he could dip his tongue into her. At once she cried out, her back arching, but he held on to her, tongue moving slowly up and down, circling, savoring her sweetness, until he felt her spasm once again, her juices flooding his mouth.

Only then did he lift his head from her, reach down so he could get rid of the tight human-made underwear that constrained him so. His tip touched her—and then she startled and backed away, scooting up toward the pillows.

He frowned, wondering what on earth was wrong. Surely she was not the kind of woman to tease him into giving her pleasure, only to back away when he wished to complete the act.

"Protection?" she said in a near-whisper, her big blue eyes meeting his, imploring.

Of course. Sarah thought he was human, and therefore could get her with child. She had no way of knowing that a djinn had to consciously decide to get a woman pregnant, that there were no "accidents" among his kind.

"Sure," he replied, then made a show of reaching over the side of the bed so he could retrieve his discarded jeans. He didn't have any condoms actually hidden within his pants pockets, but she did not have to know that. A flick of his fingers, and a foil-wrapped packet appeared within them. This would not be quite as pleasurable with the prophylactic in place, but he knew he needed it if things were to progress any further.

Moving quickly, he slid the condom over his shaft, then tossed the empty wrapper onto the nightstand, so Sarah might see it and be reassured.

"Better?" he murmured as he went to position himself between her legs again.

"Yes," she said. As if to atone for stopping him mid-flow, so to speak, she reached down and wrapped her fingers around him, moving her hand up and down slowly.

Ah, yes. The condom didn't muffle the sensations as much as he'd feared it might, and he went even harder as she stroked him—but carefully, as though she knew to be careful so he wouldn't spill his seed prematurely. After a few moments, he realized he couldn't hold off for much longer, and pulled away, needing to enter her, to feel her surround him.

That was it. He had, of course, made love to other women over the long centuries of his life, and yet there was something different about the way Sarah felt, about how the familiar act suddenly became new again. Her body began to move with his as they fell into a rhythm together, with a delicious slowness at first, and then more and more frenzied until the blessed moment when he let go, the release exquisite, perfect. He held on to her, watched her eyes shut as another climax rippled its way through her as well.

Even when it was over, he did not want to

let go. Not yet. He clung to her, listened as her breathing began to slow, then became calm and sure. Her eyes opened, wondering, yet filled with a sort of astonished affection.

"That was…." she began, then stopped, as though she didn't quite know which adjective she wished to use.

"Perfect," he said. He kissed her gently on the forehead, then on her cheek, marveling at the delicate texture of her skin.

"You're perfect," she replied.

"Mr. Perfect."

That comment made her chuckle. Kamal kissed her again, then pulled out slowly, eliciting another gasp from her. Luckily, the bathroom was only a few paces away; he climbed off the bed and discarded the condom, then cleaned himself up as best he could. At least now he didn't have to worry about Sarah questioning the running water.

When he returned, he was slightly disappointed to see that she'd already gotten dressed again. Or rather, she'd pulled on a tank top, along with her underpants. The ensemble still showed enough of her form that he decided it was probably better not to protest. Instead, he reclaimed his own briefs from where they lay on the floor and put them back on. Afterward, he climbed under the covers and snuggled next to her, experiencing another stir of desire when she wrapped her arms around him.

Her head resting on his shoulder, she said, "I'm glad you're here, Cam."

In that moment, he wanted more than anything to hear her say his true name, even though the one he had taken was not so very different. *Soon,* he told himself. *You still have to think of the best way to break the news to her.* He knew now that Sarah was the woman for him, that she must be his Chosen. They had time, though. He didn't want this wintry idyll to end. Once he had told her the truth, he would have to take her with him to Taos, and they would no longer be alone with one another.

Right now, however, he only had to tell her the truth. "I'm glad I found you, Sarah."

Cameron slept next to her, the steady rise and fall of his breath more comforting than she could have imagined. It should have felt strange to have someone here, after sleeping alone in this room for the past two months, and yet Sarah thought it seemed more as if he had always been there. Even after this short time together, she knew she'd never fit with anyone like she did with him.

Maybe this was the time to ponder the strangeness of the universe, to wonder what she could have possibly done to deserve survival at all, let alone with someone like Cam at her side. She wasn't so starry-eyed by awesome sex to think they still wouldn't have plenty of challenges to face in the months and years ahead, but she also wasn't quite so frightened, now that she didn't have to face the winter and the empty years all by herself.

She shifted slightly to find a more comfortable position, but as gently as she could so she wouldn't disturb the man sleeping next to her. It wasn't completely dark, because the glow from the hearth in the next room made its way in here, just enough for her to see his fine profile, the scatter of dark hair on the white pillowcase. Right then, she wanted to lean down and kiss him awake so they might make love again...but she didn't. They had plenty of time ahead of them, and it was important that they get their rest. The next day—if the weather cooperated—they'd venture out and gather those pine boughs, then come back and get warm, and work on decorating the Lodge. Christmas wouldn't be empty and dark, but full of light and laughter.

And, though she didn't want to even think the word, because that might jinx things…love.

They both slept in, long enough that a pale wintry light peeking through the curtains woke them. Cameron leaned over and kissed her, pulled her into his arms. It seemed the most natural thing in the world to find warmth in one another's bodies, to join once again— although she made sure to have him pause and put on another condom. Should she have been concerned that he was wandering around in a post-apocalyptic landscape, armed with a bunch of rubbers?

He probably just had them in his wallet, she told herself afterward. *Lord knows Seth always had a bunch on hand.* It was second nature for a lot of guys, like carrying a pack of gum. Cam hadn't mentioned a girlfriend, and Sarah hadn't asked. If he'd been with someone, then she was gone now, just like the rest of the world's population. A day might come when he'd feel comfortable talking about his past, about all the people he had lost, but she wouldn't push him. After all, they had plenty of time.

They both squeezed into the shower together to try out the new hot water. As Cameron soaped her back, Sarah had a hard time deciding what she'd missed more—hot showers, or good sex. She really couldn't say, and it didn't matter now. She had both.

Breakfast was quick, coffee and oatmeal and dried fruit. After they were done getting the pine boughs, they'd need to swing by the henhouse and see what the chickens had come up with overnight.

At least she and Cam wouldn't have to worry about the weather keeping them indoors. The sky overhead was almost painfully blue, like the world's most perfect sapphire. A few puffy white clouds floated in that blue expanse, and far off to the west, Sarah could see the familiar glint of White Sands, stark and pale against the San Andres mountain range.

It was cold, though. They bundled up and trudged through the fresh-fallen snow, their breath rising like smoke in the still air. Cameron carried a folded-up tarp for transporting the pine branches, and Sarah had a Thermos of extra coffee to keep them going.

"Did you say something about snowmobiles?" he asked after they'd gone about a hundred yards.

"There are some, but the lot where people used to rent them is at the far end of town," she replied. "Where we're going to get the pine branches is actually a lot closer."

His face fell so much that she wanted to laugh, but didn't. "Oh."

"We're almost there. It's not like I'm taking you all the way out to the forest proper."

Which she wasn't. Pine trees crowded most of the lots in Cloudcroft, and it wasn't as if they had to worry about taking foliage from someone's private property, so she'd decided all they really needed to do was go down the hill a little bit, then jog over on Wren Place, where there were some particularly nice specimens. All told, the walk was really not much more than a half-mile round trip.

Then again, trudging through freshly fallen snow was not exactly the same thing as walking blithely along a dry road. Sarah could feel her toes starting to get numb, despite the thick wool socks she wore. Well, this wasn't going to take all that long. They'd be back inside the Lodge within an hour at the most, and then they could put their feet up in front of the hearth in the lobby, and warm their toes and dry their socks.

"Over there," she told Cameron, pointing toward the property she had in mind. Pine and fir trees crowded thickly there, in varying sizes and heights. No worries about having to reach low-hanging branches here, that was for sure.

"Got it," he said, then stopped so he could take the tarp he held and unfold it on the snowy ground. From inside his jacket, he produced the clipping shears they'd taken from the maintenance shed. Shears in hand, he walked over toward the trees she'd indicated. "About how much do you think we'll need?"

Sarah had been pondering this question on the walk over here. There wasn't much point to decorating the entire Lodge when it was only the two of them. But a wreath for the front doors, and swags for the fireplace in the lobby and in the bar and dining room, and garlands to wrap around the banisters of the staircase from the main floor to the second level of the hotel, which had a sort of arcade where you could look down toward the lobby. That should be plenty.

"Maybe around twelve yards' worth, give or

take," she replied. "If it turns out we need more, we can come back. But I don't think the tarp can carry much more than that anyway."

"Got it."

Cameron turned away from her so he could concentrate on cutting the first batch of branches. Sarah began to walk toward him so she could help with laying them on the tarp. It would have been better if they could both cut the boughs at the same time, but they'd only been able to find the one pair of shears. It made sense to have Cam do it since he was taller than she and could reach farther without having to shift his position.

Movement out of the corner of her eye made her pause, however. For a brief second, she had the crazy idea that another survivor had heard them and was now approaching. But then as she turned to look, she realized that their new visitor wasn't human at all.

It was a large black bear.

Apparently, it hadn't gotten the memo that it was supposed to be hibernating right about now. The bear shuffled toward her, and Sarah went stock still. She knew that running was the worst thing she could do.

"Cam," she called out, her voice a desperate whisper.

He looked toward her, smiling…a smile that faded as soon as he caught sight of the enormous animal. Lowering his shears, he murmured, "Don't move."

"I won't."

A nod, but she could tell he was doing his best to avoid any sudden movements, anything that might put the animal on alert. For herself, Sarah was cursing her carelessness in not bringing her gun along on this little expedition. She'd been so wrapped up in her plans with Cam, she'd completely forgotten the precautions she'd been taking for the past two months.

Well, there wasn't much she could do about it now, except vow to never be so stupid again. Maybe the pistol wouldn't have been enough to stop a charging bear, but it certainly would have been better than nothing.

For a long, awful moment, both she and Cameron remained stock still, both of them watching the bear to see what it would do. At first it seemed to take very little notice of either one of them, was intent on snuffling around the base of a tall fir tree. What it might be smelling,

Sarah had no idea. All the dogs had disappeared from Cloudcroft months ago, around the same time all the people were dying. However, she got the impression the animals hadn't been affected by the Heat; it wasn't as though she'd seen little dog-sized piles of gray dust around town. No, it was more as if something had called them away, although she couldn't begin to guess who or what it might have been.

But if it wasn't the scent of dogs that preoccupied the bear, there had to be something else attracting it. Breath held, she watched as the bear gave up its sniffing of the one tree that had fascinated it, then moved on to a stump. However, the stump didn't appear to hold much interest, because after another minute, the animal stopped smelling around and looked straight at Sarah.

Oh, shit.

She really didn't know what else she was supposed to do. Already her feet had begun to feel like blocks of ice as she stood there, unmoving, in the snow. She couldn't hold her breath forever. And Cam was a few yards away, too far to be of much use. Not that she really knew what he could do to help.

Since she'd already been holding her breath,

it couldn't exactly strangle in her throat. Something seemed to choke her, though, as the bear let out a low growl, then went up on its hind legs before dropping back down to a crouch. And then it charged.

A scream was halfway out her throat before she realized that the bear wasn't the only thing moving. Behind it was a steep incline where the property sloped up to the next street above them. Out of nowhere, the half foot of snow that coated the hillside began to flow, going faster and faster, an avalanche that seemed to coalesce into a moving mountain, headed straight for the bear.

It didn't have a chance. The enormous mound of snow barreled right into the animal, knocking it off its feet and carrying it along in its relentless path, away from her and down the hill. Hand to her mouth, Sarah looked over at Cam in terror before she realized he wasn't in any imminent danger, that the snow mountain and its victim had been swept harmlessly past.

And as she looked at Cameron, she noticed something very odd. He had his hands raised, was making strange pushing motions, motions that seemed to echo the path of the mound of snow. The air glowed around him, blue-white, shimmering down his shoulders and arms. It was only after the bear had disappeared from sight that Cam lowered his arms. His chest raised and lowered, as though he had just run a hard mile.

Staring at him, Sarah could think of only one thing. She didn't know how it was possible, but Cameron had called the snow to protect her from the bear.

"What...?" Her voice came out all scratchy and hoarse, rough with anxiety. She cleared her throat and tried again. "What *are* you?"

Chapter Eight

As soon as Kamal saw the bear begin to advance on Sarah, he'd known what he must do. At the same time, a wave of dread swept over him. He must save her…but in the process he would be forced to reveal himself.

Unfortunately, he had no other options available to him.

Snow was water, and so would obey his command. It was a simple enough thing to make the drifts on the hillside above them flow like liquid and move to carry the bear away. The poor animal probably had no idea what was happening to it, and he did his best to make sure that it would come to no permanent harm. However, Sarah's safety was paramount. Everything else came a distant second.

He had steeled himself against her inevitable response, but even so, the words of her frightened question were like spears to his heart. Not "who are you"?

What are you?

"I am a djinn," he said quietly.

She stared at him, her expression a mixture of fear and sudden annoyance. "A *what?*"

"What your people sometimes called a genie."

No response at first. Sarah continued to stare at him with those wide, unbelieving eyes, as though she next expected him to sprout wings, or possibly turn green. "You look like an ordinary person."

"You perhaps were expecting a genie to be a large blue bald man?"

"I...." The word trailed off, hanging in the air between them. She looked so positively upset, so betrayed, that Kamal wanted nothing more than to go to her and pull her close, tell her that this changed absolutely nothing between them. He didn't, however. Somehow he knew that if he attempted to put his arms around her, she would only do her best to get herself free of him. Even though she was afraid.

Now he noticed that she was shaking, although he didn't know whether those tremors were caused by the emotion that had overcome her, or simply by standing there too long in the snow. Either way, he thought it best for her to get inside before she became truly chilled. "You're shivering," he said, his tone as gentle as he could make it. "Let me take you inside."

"I'm not going anywhere with you!" she burst you. "You—you're not even *human!* You *lied* to me! And last night—" She broke off there, as if it had just come home to her, as if she had just realized that she'd allowed herself to be intimate with someone from a strange and alien race. One gloved hand went to her throat. "How could you not tell me?"

"Well, considering the way you are currently reacting, I think most people would understand the reason for my reticence."

That retort made her delicate features go still and cold. A spot of color burned high on each cheekbone. When she spoke, her voice sounded considerably calmer, although it, too, was as chilly as the wintry December morning.

"That doesn't change the fact that you lied to me. So just—just leave me alone. Go back to wherever you came from. Just get the hell out of Cloudcroft."

A flicker of irritation moved through him. While he could understand why she might be angry, she clearly had no idea what she was asking of him. "I can't do that. It would not be safe." Should he tell her about the other djinn, the ones who had made it their goal to wipe out all traces of humanity, save for those who were Chosen? No, better not. He feared she would think he was only trying to frighten her into obedience. There should be time. Those djinn would not be done with clearing out the cities for a good while yet. Tiny Cloudcroft might not even be on their collective radar.

He hoped.

"I was fine before you came along. I'll be fine after you're gone. So get out."

Having delivered this ultimatum, she turned away from him and began trudging through the snow, headed back toward the Lodge. All Kamal had to do was reach out with his powers and immobilize her so she could go no further...but he did not. He knew an action such as that would only make her that much angrier. Better to let her go, allow her time to cool down and accept who he was. Sooner or later, he would have had to tell her the truth anyway. He only wished he could have done so on his own terms.

"I'm leaving," he said quietly. She kept moving, head down, hands curled into fists as she followed the trail they'd already broken through the snow, and gave no sign that she had heard him.

"...but I'll be back."

No crying. If she cried, her tears might freeze and stick to her eyelashes, and that would be a hell of a lot more uncomfortable than the quiet shattering of her heart.

Oh, don't be a drama queen, she told herself in some irritation. *You've only known the guy for a couple of days, and you slept with him once. How can your heart be breaking when you weren't even in love with him?*

Problem was, she thought she might have been in love with him. Or at least was beginning to be. And now it turned out he wasn't even human.

A djinn. What in the ever-loving *hell?*

She'd always prided herself on being matter-of-fact, a realist. No head in the clouds for Sarah Wells, that was for sure. No fairies and fancies and unicorns. She lived close enough to Roswell, but she didn't believe in little green men, either. Grey men. Whatever.

But now Cameron was saying he was a djinn, something out of Aladdin, or Scheherazade, or whatever. He didn't look like a genie. He looked like...well, a man. An extremely good-looking man, but still. It wasn't as if he had scales or horns or something.

Well, of course he didn't. He was a djinn, not a demon, although, if pressed, she wasn't sure she could have explained the difference between the two in any sort of a coherent manner. The supernatural was not a subject she'd studied or cared anything about, except when it came to telling tourists the story of the Lodge's resident ghost.

She stomped up the front steps of the hotel, barely pausing to knock the snow off her boots before she went inside and locked the doors behind her. Would those locks even make a difference? Cameron's display a few moments earlier hinted of powers she couldn't begin to guess at. For all she knew, he could pop right into the building without even touching a doorknob.

And she kind of doubted "Cameron" was his real name. Just another lie he'd given her. Everything was a lie, wasn't it? He didn't come from Roswell. He sure as hell wasn't some kind of working-class former ranch hand without the money for piano lessons. Nothing he'd told her was real.

Last night...had that been real? Right then she wished with all her heart that it wasn't, that she'd only dreamed of him making love to her. Making love. There was a joke. Call it what it really was. Having sex. Or maybe just plain old fucking.

Thank God she'd insisted that he use a condom. Otherwise, she could be walking around with a little half-djinn embryo inside her, or at least the beginnings of one.

A shudder wracked her then, and she hurried over to the couch so she could sit down, fearing her trembling knees might not support her for much longer. Her fingers shook so hard, she could barely undo the laces on her snow-soaked boots. Eventually, though, she got them off and set them on the hearth to dry. The fire had burned low, but it still gave off enough warmth that it would speed up the drying process. Worse come to worst, she had a spare pair in her room, but these ones were more comfortable.

As if any of that mattered. She wasn't planning on going anywhere.

Angry as she was at him, she couldn't help but wonder exactly where Cameron had disappeared to. Somewhere else in New Mexico, or to some otherworldly plane altogether?

There was just so damn much she didn't know. Somehow she doubted she would ever find out.

"You cannot leave her there like that," Zahrias said, a formidable frown knitting his brow.

"You think I do not know that?" Kamal sent a glare of his own at the leader of the djinn community in Taos, nestled in the Rio Grande valley of northern New Mexico. Because he'd returned to the resort town without his Chosen, he'd been compelled to give Zahrias an account of what had happened. The wound was raw enough that he had no fondness for the task, but at least Kamal did not have to worry about being accused of hiding something. "I cannot bear to think what might happen to her if one of the other djinn were to find her. Still, Cloud-croft is a small and obscure place. There is no reason to think that anyone would be seeking to cleanse the town so soon. Not when there are so many other places that can yield richer hunting."

Zahrias' mouth thinned. Kamal sometimes wondered about the other djinn, why he had agreed to lead this community when he had taken no Chosen of his own. It did not seem as if all his beliefs aligned with those he had volunteered to rule. But those were questions that must wait until another day. Kamal had quite enough on his own mind right now. He had come to Taos, to the house that had been given to him—and which he had hoped he would share with Sarah—but had been there no more than a half hour before the summons to this interview had arrived.

Little flickers of worried flame appeared

around Zahrias' head, indicating that the fire elemental was displeased with Kamal's response. "You say that she must surely be overlooked, and yet her safety cannot be guaranteed. Not completely. You must return and bring her here."

"She is very angry with me."

"With good reason. I had a feeling this gambit of yours would fail miserably. But if you want her—"

"I do," Kamal broke in. Never mind that if glances were blades, those looks Sarah had shot in his direction would have pierced him multiple times. In that moment as the bear approached her, he had realized how terrible it would be to lose her now, when he was so close to making her his forever. Truly, he could not have borne it. "Now more than ever, I think."

"Then you must go to her. Do whatever you have to in order to convince her that you are sorry, that this 'disguise' of yours was not intended to hurt her."

"Yes, Zahrias." As he spoke, an idea began to form in Kamal's mind. Yes, Sarah was angry —and hurt, and betrayed—and yet he thought he might have a way of reaching out to her, of proving to her that he truly did care, and wanted nothing more than to make her happy.

But to make it really work, he would have to wait until dark....

The solar panels, the hookup to the water pump —it had also been a lie. The first sign that something was wrong was when Sarah went to the bathroom to splash some water on her face. She hoped that doing so would help her come back to herself, allow her to focus on what she should do next.

Only, when she turned the handle, nothing came out of the tap. Not in her bathroom, not in the kitchen, not in the public restroom next to the gift shop. Frowning, she'd retrieved her spare boots, since the ones she'd worn that morning were still damp, then went out to check on the solar panels. Maybe they'd gotten knocked down in the storm, or the connections had somehow pulled loose.

Everything appeared intact at first glance— until she moved closer, really looked at the wires. They'd been attached to the solar panels with black electrical tape, but they weren't attached to any inputs or leads, as far as she could tell. The whole setup looked like it had been patched together to fool the casual observer.

The casual observer being her, of course. What other powers had he been hiding?

Anger lanced through her, and she stomped back into the hotel, not even caring about the mud she tracked in. By that point, the sun was high enough in the sky that it had begun to melt the snow, and large patches of soggy earth had appeared. In a way, that was good. It meant she'd find it easier to get around.

Because she didn't want Cameron—or whatever his real name was—coming back to Cloudcroft to plead with her. The storm had been a wakeup call. She needed to get out of here. Maybe there weren't any people left down the hill...but maybe there were. If she didn't at least try to find out, she knew the question would haunt her forever. Besides, if she busied herself with getting away from this place, she wouldn't have the time to wonder what the djinn had really wanted from her.

Her anger allowed her to ignore her scruples about taking someone else's vehicle, even if the owner of said vehicle had now been dead for more than two months. Oscar Martinez had owned one of the nicest trucks in town, a big Dodge Ram that wasn't even a year old. Four-wheel drive, skid plates to protect the undercarriage, the works. Even if some rocks had spilled across the highway, which they had a tendency to do in bad weather, she figured that truck could get around them. Or over them, as the case may be.

She packed her clothes, packed all the food and supplies she thought she'd need, much of which she was able to procure from the camping store in town. This felt even more like stealing than taking the truck, but again, Eric, the store's owner, wasn't going to need any of this stuff. Ditto for his former customers. By the time she was done, dusk had crept over Cloudcroft. Too late to start down the hill, even in as capable a vehicle as this one. She'd have to park it in the shed at the hotel, and then head out in the morning. Well, one more night here wouldn't kill her. She could say goodbye to the place, make her farewells to Rebecca the ghost —if she even existed—and then start fresh as soon as the sun was up.

No worries about bears, either; she had both her pistol and her rifle on the passenger seat beside her. A precaution she hadn't needed, apparently, since she hadn't seen anything bigger than a raven since she set out on this little expedition. If that bear had survived Cameron's attack, then it seemed to have fled to the hills.

Smart bear.

Sarah wound up the road that led to the Lodge, high beams on to show her the way. At least the snow hadn't returned. The sky overhead was clear, the first stars showing in the heavens already startlingly bright.

Then she came around the bend that opened on the hotel's driveway, and stomped on the brakes.

White fairy lights glittered in the trees. More white lights framed every window, and outlined the eaves. Far above, on top of the cupola where she used to keep vain watch, hoping against hope that someone might finally appear and tell her she wasn't alone in the world, glittered a bright five-pointed star.

What in the world…?

Fingers clenched on the steering wheel, she started moving slowly toward the building. As she drew closer, she saw someone standing on the front steps.

No, not just someone. Cameron.

He looked very different. Gone were the jeans and the hoodie and the T-shirt. Now he wore a long, open robe made of what looked like silk, and full pantaloons and boots. A thick silver bracelet gleamed on each wrist.

Djinn clothes? It sure looked that way.

Sarah put the truck in park and killed the engine. Heart beating with irrational strength in her chest, she got out of the cab and closed the door behind her. A step toward the djinn, then another. She stopped when she was a yard or so away, then glanced past him to the hotel, now glittering in holiday splendor.

"Your work?" she asked, since she didn't know what else to say.

"Yes," he replied. An evening wind caught at the hem of his robe, causing the silk to billow and flutter. With the sun down, it was now bitterly cold, but he didn't seem to notice, even with that distractingly bare chest and stomach. "I need to talk to you."

"What if I don't want to talk to you?"

"Please."

The word was said simply, but even in her anger, she could hear the need, the pleading behind it. Anyway, he was blocking the door.

She wasn't sure what he would do if she tried to get around him, but she also didn't think she really wanted to find out. Better to let him say his piece and then go. If he really wanted to overpower her, there wasn't much she could do to stop him.

"Fine," she said grudgingly. "Don't think you're going to change my mind, though."

He inclined his head. "I only want to talk."

She shrugged, hoping the apparent nonchalance of the gesture would hide the tension roiling within her. "All right. Come inside."

The door was still locked, just as she'd left it. She unclipped the carabiner with its set of hotel keys from her belt and inserted the one that opened the deadbolt on the front door. It was only as the door began to swing inward that she realized it had been adorned with a wreath, one with a big red bow on it.

The second thing she noticed was that the interior of the hotel was not dark, as she'd been expecting, but lit by the sconces on the walls and the heavy wrought-iron chandelier that hung in the center of the lobby. Adding to the illumination was an enormous fir tree, set off to one side of the lobby. White twinkling lights covered all of its ten feet and more, and ornaments gleamed within its branches. A fire danced in the hearth, and on the table was a decanter filled with rich red wine, and a plate of cheese and crusty bread and fresh fruit, the sort of thing she hadn't tasted in months.

She turned back toward Cameron, who had closed the door behind him and stood there with a watchful expression on his face, as though observing her to see how she would react to the sudden appearance of all this Christmas cheer. "You did this?"

He nodded.

"All of it? Just while I was gone?"

"Yes. It was really not all that much work."

For a djinn, maybe. Sarah remembered how it had taken five people working three days straight to decorate the Lodge last holiday season. What, did he just have to snap his fingers to make all this appear?

"It looks beautiful," she allowed, and something in his posture relaxed slightly.

"I am glad you like it. Come, you must be hungry. Let us sit down and talk."

And get me tipsy so I'm all suggestible and forgiving, she thought. *Sorry, not happening.* Even so, she knew she wanted to hear what he had to say, wanted to hear his explanations. Maybe then she'd have some answers to the questions that had been plaguing her all day.

"All right," she said.

They both seated themselves on the couches. Sarah was relieved to see that the djinn didn't try to sit next to her, and instead took the sofa on the other side of the coffee table. He poured some wine into a pair of glasses, then reached across the table to hand one to her.

"Thank you for letting me speak to you."

"You're not going to change my mind."

"Perhaps."

He looked so self-assured. And, she was forced to admit to herself, pretty damn spectacular. Something about his dark, exotic looks was only enhanced by that getup he had on. Looking at him now, she wondered how she could have ever thought he was just a regular guy.

"What's your name?" she asked abruptly. "Your real name, I mean. Not the one you handed me."

"I am Kamal," he replied. "Kamal al-Sayid."

"So…you're from Saudi Arabia or something?"

"No. Djinn names sound like the given

names from that part of the world, but I assure you, my people lived there long before there was a Saudi Arabia, or any of the other nations in that region."

There really wasn't anything reassuring about any of this, but still, Sarah was oddly relieved to hear his real name. Kamal. It suited him. "So what's a djinn doing hanging around Cloudcroft, New Mexico?"

"To be with you, of course."

"Me?" She raised an eyebrow. "Am I supposed to be flattered that a supernatural being wanted to get in my pants?"

He didn't look offended by the remark. Instead, he smiled slightly, as though remembering exactly what it had been like to get in those pants. "You misunderstand. I chose you to be my partner."

"Chose me? Why? Did you get tired of djinn women or something?" *If there even are djinn women,* she added mentally. *I have no idea how any of this is supposed to work.*

"No. That is, whether or not I am weary of them has nothing to do with why I chose you. I knew that you would be one of those who would survive the Dying, and I also knew that I wanted you to be the one who would come to share my life."

Survive the Dying.... Her eyes narrowed. "You mean you *knew* this was going to happen? The end of the world?"

"The end of *your* world," he corrected her, although his tone was kind, and the dark eyes that held hers concerned, almost gentle. "The djinn created the Heat so they might take back this world. Because they created the disease, they also knew who would survive."

Oh, God. Sarah didn't even realize she'd gotten to her feet until she found herself standing, her entire body taut with fury. "*You* did this? You killed everyone?"

"No, *I* did not. There is a small group of us who disagreed, who thought the creation of the Heat was an abomination. There weren't enough of us to stop it, unfortunately. All we could do was get the assurance that the mortals we selected as our partners would be safe. This is why I chose you, Sarah. I had to make sure no harm would ever come to you."

The room seemed to be spinning around her, the lights from the Christmas tree swirling like some kind of mad, out-of-control carousel. She began to lift a hand to her forehead, hoping the pressure might help to stop this sudden rush of vertigo. At once Kamal was there beside her. His hands reached for hers, holding them tight, giving her a center to focus on.

No…she couldn't let him touch her. He was evil. Or…was he? He'd said that he wanted to save her, protect her.

She didn't understand any of this.

"I know it is a great deal to take in," he murmured, still grasping her fingers. "And you have every right to be angry. I am angry, too, at what my people did. Please know that not all of us are like that. Truly, we are not."

She blinked and made herself look up at him. His dark eyes were earnest, beseeching her to understand, to believe him. How could she, though? He'd already lied to her.

"Why didn't you tell me from the beginning?" she asked at last, her voice barely for than a scratchy whisper. "What was the point of all those lies?"

"Ah, Sarah." He pulled her to him, and for some reason, she didn't resist. Call her crazy, but it felt good to have those strong arms go around her and hold her close, almost as though she was supposed to be there next to him. "That was my own foolishness. I had chosen you, but I wished to know you better. I wanted you to treat me as one of your own kind, rather than a djinn. I thought...I thought if you could love Cameron, who was no one terribly special, then you would also love Kamal, would realize we were one and the same, at least at heart. I know now that I made a terrible mistake. It was wrong of me to mislead you. All I can do now is ask your forgiveness."

How could she forgive him? He'd lied repeatedly...and even though he claimed to be innocent, he'd just admitted how his people had created the plague that destroyed the world, the terrible disease that killed her father and everyone else she knew.

"You don't deserve it," she whispered.

His jaw tightened, but to her surprise, he only nodded. "You are right. I don't deserve for you to forgive me. I can only hope that you are kind enough, gracious enough...noble enough...to give me that which I don't deserve."

Kind...gracious...noble...was she worthy of any of those adjectives? She didn't know. No one had ever called her any of those things before, just as no one had ever spoken to her like this before. So earnest, so troubled, so passionate.

But….

When she looked deep within, she understood then that she couldn't hate Kamal. He had admitted to his mistake. She'd known people who would never, ever admit that they'd screwed up. Even her own father would never acknowledge that it might have been better for both of them if they'd left Cloudcroft, rather than stay here and hang on to memories of someone who'd abandoned them years earlier.

But Kamal had made that admission. He'd stood there and confessed to his wrongdoing. That had to count for something, didn't it?

As for the rest…she didn't even know what to think about that. Surely he couldn't agree with what the other djinn had done, or he wouldn't be here with her now. He would have sought her death from the very moment he laid eyes on her.

"How many djinn think like you?" she asked at last.

He let out a breath, as if relieved that she had set aside her anger enough to ask the question. "We are called the One Thousand, because that is our number. There are some fifty of us in Taos right now, with our human partners."

A thousand djinn, out of how many? Did it matter, though? What mattered was at least there were a thousand of these beings who believed humans were worth saving, who had defied what the majority wanted. A thousand djinn meant a thousand humans saved.

There were so many other things she wanted to know, but she supposed she would come to learn more in the days and weeks and months ahead. More about who these djinn really were, what their powers might be. She'd caught a glimpse of those powers in Kamal, in the way he'd protected her from the bear, and how he'd been able to give her hot running water here at the hotel. Well, that was something. Sarah had a feeling she wouldn't be lacking for creature comforts in her new home.

"And is that where you want to take me? Up to Taos?"

"Yes." His arms tightened around her, and she felt him brush a kiss against the top of her head. "It is the only place I can take you. That is part of the agreement—that we of the One Thousand live in our own communities with our Chosen, away from the rest of the djinn."

Taos. She'd never been there. A resort town to the north, in a high valley ringed with mountains. It would be a new adventure. One of many, she supposed.

Well, she *had* been trying to get out of Cloudcroft....

Very gently, she pressed her lips to the bare skin of his chest, then pulled away. She knew she'd already made her decision. "All right. That is, I think I forgive you. Maybe I'm crazy, but—"

She never got the chance to finish, for Kamal bent to kiss her, his mouth warm, insistent. A flush of desire passed over her, shocking, sudden. Obviously, her body was ready to forgive him, too.

When the kiss ended, she caught the mischievous flash of Kamal's eyes and glanced upward. Hanging from the center of the chandelier was a large sprig of mistletoe, bound with red ribbon.

"You do think of everything, don't you?"

"I try," he replied. "And we shall still have our Christmas here, before I take you away to Taos. Would you like that?"

She nodded. "I would. I think it would help —having a chance to really say goodbye to everything."

"Then you will have your chance. And we will start the new year in our new home."

His arms went around her again, and she lifted her mouth to receive his kiss. He took her to the couch and handed a glass of wine to her. They toasted one another, and broke bread, and relaxed into one another's company, while the white lights glittered on the Christmas tree he'd brought for her, and the portrait of Rebecca smiled at them from the foyer, a little sad, as though she knew she would soon be the only one left here, a ghost town without a true ghost.

But it would be a new beginning for Sarah and Kamal, and perhaps the world. A way for her to move forward, with the djinn who loved her at her side. And in the meantime, the past she remembered could shine brightly one last time, before its illumination was gone forever.

The End

This is the final book of the Djinn Wars series, but a spin-off series, Djinn Dominion, is coming in April 2018.

Sign up for Christine Pope's newsletter so you don't miss out on any information about new releases and special sales!

THE WATCHERS TRILOGY

(Paranormal Romance)

Falling Dark

Dead of Night

Rising Dawn

THE WITCHES OF CLEOPATRA HILL

(Paranormal Romance)

Darkangel

Darknight

Darkmoon

Sympathetic Magic

Protector

Spellbound

A Cleopatra Hill Christmas

Impractical Magic

Strange Magic

The Arrangement

Defender

Bad Blood

Deep Magic

Darktide

THE DJINN WARS

(Paranormal Romance)

Chosen

Taken

Fallen

Broken

Forsaken

Forbidden

Awoken

Illuminated

THE SEDONA FILES

(Paranormal Romance)

Bad Vibrations

Desert Hearts

Angel Fire

Star Crossed

Falling Angels

Enemy Mine

TALES OF THE LATTER KINGDOMS

(Fantasy Romance)

All Fall Down

Dragon Rose

Binding Spell

Ashes of Roses

One Thousand Nights

Threads of Gold

The Wolf of Harrow Hall

Moon Dance

The Song of the Thrush

THE GAIAN CONSORTIUM SERIES

(Science Fiction Romance)

About the Author

Christine Pope has been writing stories ever since she commandeered her family's Smith-Corona typewriter back in the sixth grade. Her work includes paranormal romance, fantasy romance, and science fiction/space opera romance. She fell under the Land of Enchantment's spell while researching her Djinn Wars series and now makes her home in Santa Fe, New Mexico.

To be notified about new releases by Christine Pope, please go to www.christinepope.com and sign up for her newsletter.